Becoming Lilith

"The One"

DEDICATION

D.P. Brown…What can I say but Thank You! You kept asking me about my writing and finally lit the spark. Your encouragement and push helped me find my passion for writing again. And for being on the same literary wavelength. He is an amazing author. He has romance, fantasy, thriller, and scifi works out there! You won't be disappointed.

My Husband…You gave me love, life, and a chance at my dreams. Because of you I have achieved so much more than I could have ever imagined. Eternity does not feel long enough to have you in my world. I love you more than I can ever express.

K and **M**…You two have made being a mother the excitement of a lifetime. You have given life purpose and challenge. I love you both more than you will ever know. I hope you both know how proud I am of you.

Z…Giving you a life with two people who love you was the hardest and greatest decision I could have made. God blessed me and your parents with an angel who gave us an insurmountable amount of joy and love. Finding you was the final piece of my journey and I am so grateful everyday to have you in my life.

D and B…Thank you for the love you showed a tragic teenage girl and her son. You will never know the amount of peace and gratitude I have for the both of you. Your joy and letters brought me through some of my darkest days. Z and I were both blessed to have you in our lives.

My Dearest and Bestest Friends...who are like my sisters: Thank you for supporting me. For listening to me talk about all the changes and for encouraging me to push forward. Thank you for reading this as I went along, giving me pointers, and not judging me for the twisty nature of it. I love all of you so much.

My Grandchildren...being your Mimi will always be the most cherished role I will ever fill. I never saw myself as a "grandmother" and yet the three of you pulled me into your orbits and...now...I never want to leave. I look forward to watching you all grow and hopefully get to see you all have families of your own.

Charlotte Chaos... THANK YOU!! Thank you for the laughs. The snarky comments in the margins while you were editing and for making me not feel so isolated in this wonderful world of writing.

HEY READER...seriously... if you need a palette cleanser after this book... you need to check out Charlotte's series Death Defiant. It will give you all the feels! And it is full of snarky humor and hunky horseman...and one sexy horseman.

For those of us who always felt for the villain instead of the hero/heroine…

This book is for you!

****<u>FAIR WARNING: The content you are about to read is not for the faint of heart. If you have any triggers…RUN.</u>****

ACKNOWLEDGMENTS

I acknowledge this book was the hardest and most difficult piece of work next to graduate school homework. I acknowledge I gave my husband many headaches yelling at both. It has been years in the making and has gone through so many rewrites that I can tell you the original story…could still be its own story.

Other works by MZ Pak:

Well none, but here is what you can expect!

Becoming Series:

Becoming Lilith "The One"

Becoming Cain "The Two"

Becoming Lucifer "The Three"

Book 4: Title TBD…Becoming…Something???

Prologue

Black and white, right and wrong, good and evil—these comforting illusions we've been fed since childhood mask a darker, more terrifying truth. What if beneath these simplistic tales lurked a sinister design, a hidden world where your fragile faith could shatter like brittle glass? Imagine a reality where evil is not what you've been led to believe, where mercy is a lie meant to force conformity, and where shadows conceal secrets too horrifying for your feeble mind to comprehend.

I once walked your path, blind to the insidious lies woven into our understanding. When the illusions shattered, what lay beneath changed me forever.

Would you brand me a heretic if I told you Adam and Eve were not the parents of humanity's first child? The Canaanites—spawn of Lilith and Caine—were merely a continuation of her dark legacy. Lilith had twins, born of two fathers: one of purest light, the other steeped in unending darkness. Lilith herself, trapped eternally between the realms of purity and corruption, painted gray by her creator's cruel whim.

One of these twins bore a soul tainted by Lucifer's vengeful hand—a twisted reflection of the divine, shaped in Lucifer's sinister image. It was his final act of defiance, a giant 'fuck you' to his father.

When God cast Lilith from Eden's sacred ground, he was oblivious to the fragile life already stirring in her womb, a child fathered by his precious Adam. Had he known, he would have confined her, waiting coldly for the birth before discarding her like refuse. Yes, the God you worship, the one you blindly trust to be merciful, is ruthless—his generosity overshadowed by his hunger to take.

Lucifer found Lilith wandering the shadowy fringes of Eden, sensing the life pulsing within her. He offered her a simple choice: lay with me and bear that which will be mine and revive the dying parasite in your womb, or be damned to walk the darkness with the lifeless unborn for eternity.

She made her choice…

Lilith's fateful decision unleashed a storm, a butterfly effect rippling through the ages; its echo, eternal. Neither human, angel, demon, nor God himself could foresee the chaos that ensued. In his fury, God desperately scrambled to erase her actions, wielding floods, fires, plagues—catastrophes born of divine tantrums, leaving humanity broken and bloody in his wake.

Throughout the endless march of history, humanity worshipped countless gods—each fading as Christianity clawed its way into dominance, feeding the eternal father's need for worship and adoration. Yet we move blindly, clutching desperately to the comforting lies of divine love and mercy. In truth, our God is nothing more than a petulant child wielding a magnifying glass, delighting in our suffering as if we were mere ants.

Legends of vampires have been twisted grotesquely through time— shifting from nightmarish, alien monstrosities to alluring beings cloaked in seduction, romance, and admiration. Now, these terrifying truths have withered into half-forgotten myths, leaving humanity vulnerable in their willful ignorance.

Lucifer's desire for Lilith was his ultimate downfall, as she ascended to become mother, lover, queen, and sacred deity to the Shedim. These beings, whose very existence defied God's tyrannical order, made their home in the abyssal darkness of Sheol, guilty only of living by their own unyielding creed. To you, fragile and naive reader, they may seem merely shadows—empty voids untouched by light— but beware, for they are infinitely more, infinitely darker, and far more horrifying than your feeble mind can grasp.

After Lilith bore her twins, offspring of Adam and the twisted twin belonging to Lucifer, she turned fully to the Shedim, shrouding herself in their eternal darkness, she roamed the earth, possessing women in their most vulnerable states—when they carried new life within. There, in the secrecy of the womb, she corrupted innocence, tainting each unborn child with a single, damning drop of her cursed blood.

Waiting for the day when her chance to rise from the shadows would come…

Chapter 1

Kallea

The air reeked of decay and vitality—a strange, cruel dance between reality's brutality and the ironic beauty I could no longer escape. The alleyway, wrapped in twilight and washed in the sickly yellow glow of flickering fluorescent bulbs, offered an illusion of safety. No one realized the shadows slithered like predators here, and I was hiding amongst them. They did not just hide me—they whispered to me.

I was no longer the woman I once knew. I looked the same, yet I didn't. Sounded the same, yet there was an edge that wasn't there before. I was me and…yet…I felt alien in my own body. I was vampire, a predator of nightmares. And it waged war with my humanity, and the only way to stop it was to die. Again.

At times, my own reflection startled me. Everything was different, darker, sinister, less…me. Even my senses were different: smell, touch, taste, sight, hearing. All magnified to serve my new found need for survival through hunting. The vampire I had become was no elegant, romantic creature from the movies. My existence was gritty, primal, and ruthless. I reveled in it when feeding. I loathed it when sated. The unending yo-yo of emotions gave me whiplash.

It felt like only a few short months since my death and then my rebirth. My eyes no longer mirrored my dreams. Instead, hunger thrived in them. The life I worked hard for was slipping away from me. I had worked as an RN in hospital corridors, planning a future in medicine. Anthony and I were to be married next summer. And it was all turning to ash in my memory. Yet, here I was the harbinger of death.

I thought of my parents. They must be absolutely devastated and worried sick about me. I knew I could not go to them, or Anthony. I could not risk losing control and attacking them. They were food now. And I didn't want them to look into my eyes and them see the thing I was now. The thing I, myself, feared.

My parents, had immigrated from Romania with my older sister when my mother was pregnant with me. My sister died just three years after my birth in a freak accident. Since then, they had been overprotective, nearly smothering me with their concern.

The American Dream laid out for me by their hard work, gone in a single instant, more rubble in the wake of my new life. Now, I was consumed by a craving for the elixir of life that flowed through all of humanity.

I waited, silent and still, crouched low within the embrace of the shadows, cloaking myself in darkness as naturally as breathing. This alley became my hunting ground and it never failed to bring me sustenance for the night. My ears perked up, listening for any noise, eyes watchful for movement, nose flaring subtly to catch the first whiff of tonight's conquest.

"Feed..." The whispers a constant and unwelcomed companion.

Chance alone decided who would cross my path, drunk or sober, it didn't matter. All that mattered was what pumped hotly beneath their skin, rich and intoxicating. All my mind knew, at this moment, was the desire to feed and hide from the sun before it peaked over the horizon.

How did I end up here?

Why did this happen to me?

Why was I sounding like one of those obnoxious romance novel girls? You know they cannot pull their heads out of their twats long enough to formulate an independent thought. I vacillated between wanting this life and hating the fact it broke every moral code I had ever known. My thoughts constantly swirled between my own and the unnatural feeling of *another* lurking in my head.

The doorknob rattled beside me, pulling me from my internal thoughts, keys jingling against each other. A tired symphony marking the end of someone's mundane shift. Then he stepped into view, young and weary wearing the stench of ash, sweat, cheap booze, and vomit like a second skin that spoke of a hard night's work. Beneath the grime, the unmistakable scent of life—sweet, vibrant, and potent—beckoned to me. My mouth watered uncontrollably, and a primal growl vibrated within my chest.

I stepped forward cautiously, deliberately, careful not to startle him prematurely. The darker part of me—a feral impulse buried deep within—relished the thought of frightening him. Fear sweetened blood in ways nothing else could, transforming a simple meal into a decadent feast. His exhausted posture and tired eyes promised he would put up little fight. His body begged for rest.

Yep, he would do. I was too hungry to care beyond the need to feed, rather than trying to 'spice' up my meal. His back was to me as he locked up for the night, oblivious to my presence. The closer I got to him, the more my mouth watered and the compulsion to feed grew, clouding my mind.

"Excuse me, sir," I purred, attempting to disguise the underlying growl of hunger. I'm sorry to bother you, but I think my friend left her keys inside. She gave them to me, or I thought she did, but now they're gone."

He paused, hesitated then turned toward me. His gaze hazy yet alert enough to assess me. A flicker of pity flashed briefly across his face, the familiar expression reserved for drunk girls, lost girls. Harmless girls. Stupid girls. How wrong he was about me, for I was none of those girls. At least the predator in me was not. I was more than I even knew.

"I don't think anyone turned any in," he offered resignation laced his voice. "But I can check. Give me a moment to disarm the alarm. Just…uh…just wait here." His gaze briefly morphed into fear before settling back to tiredness.

He turned his back, unlocking the door he just exited. My gums ached as my canines pressed forward like sharp thorns breaking skin. Contrary to myth, fangs weren't always visible; mine emerged only with hunger, transforming me into the predator I was made into without consent—without guidance. My sire had abandoned me soon after turning me, leaving me alone to navigate the harsh realities of this dark world. Hollywood lied; there was no glamour here, just the dirty reality of scavenging, and fleeting moments of dark pleasure I pretended not to savor.

I did not exude power, nor did I sparkle like diamonds. No, I fucking hid in the dark, and slept wherever I could find a place with no way for the sunlight to reach me. That shit fucking HURTS when it touches you. It took me weeks to heal from the barest of touches. Then there were the constant whispers coming from the shadows, plaguing me without end.

Impatience surged within me, growing intolerable. The cool metal doorknob twisted beneath my fingers, still warmer than my flesh, as I silently slipped inside. The hallway lay dim, illuminated only by a faint sliver of light seeping beneath a door to the left. I heard him moving around inside the room, boxes shifting, drawers opening and closing, quiet curses muttered beneath his breath. Frustration built inside him like pressure in a pipe. He would return home to accusations and suspicion despite his innocence, his wife's unfounded anger awaiting him. His frustrated sighs dancing through the air, tickling my ears.

The enticing scent of his sweat rose through the crack beneath the door, hot and vibrant, causing my senses to overload, driving me mad. I barely noticed when the door opened. His face suddenly inches from mine. His eyes widened at the sight of me…and what a sight it was, a small woman covered in dirt, grime, remnants of previous prey, and whatever else that came from living like a rat in the world.

"You shouldn't be back here," he stammered, initial confusion rapidly replaced by irritation and mounting fear. "Really, I need you to leave. I did not find any keys. I think you have the wrong bar."

I inhaled deeply, savoring the sharp, electric scent of his fear. "You smell so good," I whispered. My body trembled with barely restrained hunger. "I can hear your heart racing. Your fear—it smells like an approaching thunderstorm."

I stepped back slightly, watching the jaundiced ceiling light accentuate his features: dusty blond hair spiked with sweat, lips tight with worry, boyish dimples deepening in alarm. The pale skin of his neck pulsed, visible beneath the surface, calling to me. Tempting me. It's invitation a steady beat of promise. My famished gaze fixated on the hollows just above his collarbone, drawing me closer.

Then came the whispers—soft at first, yet rapidly growing louder, insistent, demanding.

"Drink of him."

"Take his blood."

"Feed us."

"Mistress is here."

The voices weren't just around me—they were inside me. A dark chorus amplifying my hunger, urging me toward inevitable action. I always tried to resist. Always. But seeing his genuine fear shattered my fragile control. A twisted smirk touched my lips. Lips that belonged not to the human me, but to this new version.

I lunged, my teeth sinking effortlessly into his tender flesh like sharpened knives plunging into ripe fruit, puncturing deep. Hot liquid surged heavily against my tongue, flooding my mouth with exquisite, intoxicating warmth, spilling down my chin, and spraying the room around us. He struggled desperately against my grasp, cries muffled, fists flailing weakly. It was useless; my grip was iron, my hunger relentless. His futile resistance only heightened my satisfaction, feeding my dark instincts further.

His life drained from his body. Every swallow eased the never ending hunger. His pulsed weakened until it finally ceased. The rattle of his last breath vibrated against my own chest. I held him for an extra moment, savoring the quiet stillness left behind, relishing the heavy silence punctuated only by my own harsh breathing, and the fading echoes of his final heartbeats.

I released his lifeless form gently to the floor, and stood silently over him, savoring the lingering warmth in my veins. The momentary satisfaction deepened rather than fading. His glazed eyes stared upward in perpetual horror. His mouth frozen open in an unanswered plea. His eyes glassed over, staring into the eternal abyss of the after life.

His life's essence trickled thick and dark, formed a crimson pool beneath him from the gash in his throat. The aroma added to the intoxication I was feeling. Copper mixed with his natural earthy scent. Bitter undertones mingled in as his body began to break down. It held me there, a tether of dark fascination that refused to let go.

My predatory senses, now fully awakened, were sharper and more vivid than ever before. His death wasn't merely sustenance—it was a profound, darkly beautiful act. I knelt beside him, examining my handiwork carefully, a mixture of pride and horror swirling within me. His youthful features were now slack and his skin waxen and pale, and the memory of his warm vitality contrasted cruelly with the cold emptiness he now embodied.

The shadows around us grew heavier, richer, whispering in approval. I was acutely aware of every subtle sensation: the chill of the concrete seeping into my skin, the lingering heat of his body as it faded into oblivion. I ran my fingers delicately through his dusty blond hair, tracing a slow path down his pale cheek, his neck, savoring the memory of the pulse that once held such delicious promise.

Something within me cherished this moment. Savored its perfection. Celebrated the ruthless beauty of my newfound existence. And even as I soaked in the feeling of satiation, I knew the euphoria would not last long.

A cruel curiosity filled me. His blood stained my lips and fingers. I tasted it again. The familiar addictive rush flooded through my veins. The shadows hissed with pleasure, approving of my indulgence. I leaned closer, whispering into his lifeless ear.

"Thank you," My adoration for his sacrifice laced each word. "You gave yourself to me so beautifully."

Here, with his taste still on my tongue, I felt a perverse peace. The guilt that once plagued me was now only a faint echo. I had become this creature—this predator—and it no longer repulsed me as it once had.

In this moment, I was no longer chained to my former humanity. I was free from being forced to pretend at normalcy. I belonged fully to the darkness. And in this kill, in this raw and intimate act of death, I embraced the terrifying beauty of my true nature. Though I still struggled with the lingering human guilt killing always brought. The mortal emotions were unending. A constant barrier to my acceptance of this new life.

I settled deeper into the shadows, still crouched beside my prey. I basked in the lingering taste on my tongue. The feeling of disgust began to settle into my marrow. I wanted to cry. I wanted to feel bad. The internal struggle between the monster I was becoming and the human I once was keeping me in a constant state of dissociation. Dawn still being several hours away meant I had time to flee and hide.

I hated it. Hated myself. The tears I held back began to flow as my mortal mind cleared. I cried for the loss of my life as I knew it. For this life I now had that I both loved and loathed. For my family who I would not see again. Even as I fought to keep a hold on my mind, now that I had fed, I knew the hold was precarious. I tried to only kill once in a night and even with this being the first…I would do the same to another if I let myself feed again.

I was dead inside, just as much as this bartender was dead beside me. I killed him to simply feed me, without thought as to if he had a family or not. Would his wife miss him? Did he have children? Would they miss him or would their mother spin it as though he left for milk and never came home?

Chapter 2

Vakor

I awoke at dusk, a potent cocktail of hunger and lust pulsing through me like a second heartbeat. Tonight, blood alone wouldn't satisfy—something deeper, more primal stirred within me. Sex. It wasn't often this urge seized me so intensely; only the third time in nearly thirty years.

The last occurrence had been just months ago, but the craving had returned, stronger than ever. Perhaps it was the shift of seasons, or simply the ceaseless monotony of immortality that brought these forward. Though I sensed there was more to it. I just could not put my finger on the unknown sensation.

Stretching luxuriously, I rose from the silk sheets of my oversized bed, the dark velvet drapes rustling slightly in the whisper of circulated air. Coffins? An absurd mortal myth, along with garlic, stakes, and useless mirrors.

Garlic was delightful in cuisine; mirrors flattering—I knew my reflection intimately. Every line and sinew, every curve of lean muscle that defined my immortal physique was etched in my memory. Vanity, it seemed, transcended mortality. Though—having never been mortal—I wouldn't know.

The sun, however, was true torment: Unlike the dramatic instant combustion mortals imagined, the reality prolonged agony. We didn't burst into flames instantly; instead, we smoldered painfully. Flesh split, peeled, and burned endlessly in the sunlight's merciless glare. As a creature of advanced age, it held an even greater threat. Prolonged torment instead of swift demise. Even when we fled its rays of light the burn did not stop. Sired vampires did not fare as well. It only took a few moments in the torturous light for them to smolder and burn.

Their screams lingered long after their forms dissolved. Such irony, that mortals associated daylight with safety. For creatures like me, daylight symbolized agony incarnate. Fucking God and his determination to stop anyone who did not agree with him.

I padded barefoot across the cool stone floor of my lavishly appointed chamber and flicked on my shower. Irritation settling in at the thought of that bright ball of angel essence filling the sky to keep the undesirables contained to the dark. The brushed nickel rainfall head sprang to life, enveloping the room in dense, billowing steam. Even monsters craved cleanliness and luxury—perhaps especially so. Every mortal indulgence, every decadent detail was mine to enjoy.

Before stepping beneath the warm cascade, I admired myself in the full-length antique mirror positioned perfectly in the corner of the spacious bathroom. Youthful perfection stared back at me—a flawless golden tan, carefully maintained by regular applications of sunless lotion, accentuated the stark beauty of my raven-black hair and eyes of molten amber.

My sculpted physique, enhanced and refined over countless centuries, remained the ultimate temptation for mortals desperate enough to seek forbidden thrills. My reflection hid a ruthless predator, eternally patient, an invitation to irresistible doom. With calculated intent, I allowed my fangs to descend, sharp and deadly. Mortals never noticed their lethal presence until it was too late. Their blind ignorance was almost poetic.

But vampires weren't the only creatures of the night stalking through the darkness. We were merely the boldest, walking brazenly through shadows while other, lesser creatures skulked fearfully in hidden corners. Lycans, witches, and other supernatural entities existed, but none carried themselves with the unapologetic superiority we vampires exuded. They stayed sheltered away from the human realm, not wanting to deal with their unending bullshit.

Lately, however, even the shadows themselves had grown restless. They whispered dark urgings. Something was shifting. I felt it deep in my bones. Fear, though, never touched me. After myriads of existence, fear was a foreign sensation. Yet, there was something foreboding in the air disrupting the hidden. While I did not fear it, I knew well enough to be cautious moving forward.

The hot water hit my skin, usually soothing, but tonight it only heightened my growing lust. My cock throbbed painfully, demanding immediate attention. I wrapped my hand around its firm length, stroking gently at first, then with increased urgency as vivid memories surged forth, fueling the ache within.

That night, months ago, the moon hid behind thick clouds, plunging the city into merciful darkness. A storm presented a light show far in the distance, the wind whirled through the trees, and the air smelled of life, death, and nature. The faint sounds of the city below cutting through the loudness of the wind whipping through my hair.

I had been heading toward my favorite hunting ground, Oíche Cheiliúrtha—a bar whose patrons celebrated distraction rather than joy, inebriation instead of lucidity, and lost inhibitions instead of control. On that particular night, however, fate had intervened. I'd caught the unmistakable scent of smoke, oil, and blood—a cocktail irresistible to creatures like myself.

I found the source—a crashed '77 VW Beetle. It was half consumed by fire. It had gone down the embankment and was barely held by a large tree. The woman driver's faint moans reached my ears, almost inaudible even to my heightened senses.

"Help... please," she whispered, her voice a fragile, desperate thing.

A predatory smile crept onto my lips—an appetizer before the main course.

The flames had threatened the vehicle's backseat as I moved swiftly, silently, cutting her free and pulling her limp body from the wreckage. Blood painted her face like a crimson veil, mingling grotesquely with ash and tears. "Thank you—" she had managed to murmur, then fell silent, unconscious.

I could hear the internal bleeding beneath her skin. It hastened her inevitable demise. Her time was limited to mere moments with the severity of her injuries. I could hear the pulse of the aneurysm beneath her skull. The grind of broken bones accompanying the symphony of death.

I showed her mercy. My fangs pierced her jugular. Her blood fiery sweet, intoxicating against my tongue, and yet, there was something I could not quite pinpoint in her taste. Something…familiar. Her sudden awakening, thrashing and panicked, only heightened my arousal. Her skin tore where my fangs had pierced. The primal terror in her struggles fueled my hunger.

I tore away her clothing as desire surged forward, driving myself deeply into her warm, struggling body. Each desperate pulse of her heartbeat combined with my thrusting, pushed fresh blood into my mouth, and the rhythm of her terror carried me rapidly toward the edge of release. Even as headlights approached in the distance, illuminating our final, grotesque dance, I found no reason to pause.

"Hey! Everything alright down there?" a distant mortal voice called just as her heart began to slow and I spilled hotly inside her. The ultimate climax of blood and pleasure.

I was so lost in the euphoria and pleasure that I did not see the human male come down next to us. "What the fuck are you doing to her? Get the fuck off her you sick pervert."

The impact of a large branch hitting the side of my face, jarred me. The inside of my cheeks split at impact against my razor sharp teeth. My blood mixed with the woman's blood that I still held in my arms. Rage immediately coated me like an exoskeleton, shimmering under the pale luminescence of the flashlight he held. My growl radiating from deep within my chest, crashing through my tightly pulled blood smeared lips. This human would die tonight too.

"Wha...wha...what the fuck are you?" The last words he said as I dropped the woman's husk and lunged at the male. My fangs hit his jugular straight on, blood rushed into my mouth. Ran down my chin. It soaked my tank top and jeans. When I was satisfied and had my fill, I tossed his empty shell into the now fully engulfed car, leaving him to burn. I stared down at her. Her heartbeat faint as it slowed, signaling her impending death.

A guttural groan left my my lips as I climaxed at the memory. My forehead rested against the stone wall of my shower as the last vestiges of my orgasm and the memory faded. There was something about that woman I could not shake and I felt a twinge of regret for not just turning her. She could have been a useful companion.

I almost felt bad for killing him considering how bold he was attacking me in the middle of feeding and fucking. Though a little credit was due since he had no idea who or what I was, which made his heroics all the more humorous.

The memory fueled my hunger now, intensifying the ache. I scrubbed myself faster, trying to quicken my shower, but it did little to ease the urgency. I grabbed the towel next to me, running it over me as

I strode to my massive closet. My usual choice of clothing, tight Gucci jeans and a pristine white tank top. Garments meant to entice and warn simultaneously. Humans would be drawn to me. Their lack of self preservation made them unable to resist the fatal attraction.

I worshipped my immortality. My long existence had allowed me to accumulate unimaginable wealth and unparalleled power. My vast fortune spanned continents, guarded carefully under countless aliases. The IRS, and indeed every institution of human control, rested comfortably in my pocket. Mortals were puppets, blissfully ignorant of the strings manipulating their lives.

I entered the garage, where my midnight black 2015 Mustang Cobra waited. A sleek predator on wheels. The engine purred beneath my touch as it roared to life. A powerful beast hungry for the thrill of the hunt. I peeled onto the winding road. The wind screamed around me. It brought with it promises of a fruitful night. Tonight, the beast within would feast—on blood, on flesh, on unbridled pleasure.

The city lights blurred past. Humans went about their lives oblivious, unaware of the true apex predators moving freely among them. They thought themselves safe, comforted by the illusion of control and civilization. It amused me greatly—their arrogance, their ignorance, their hopeless vulnerability.

Time had allowed me to observe human history. The rise and fall of civilizations. The futile attempts at control and order. Yet, beneath their carefully constructed societies, darkness thrived. Mortals believed themselves above primal instincts. Yet they sought constantly to indulge them in secret. Their shame kept them hidden from judgmental eyes. Their hypocrisy provided endless entertainment.

As I drove through the city streets, the scents of humanity bombarded me. A chaotic symphony of life and desperation. Each mortal carried a unique flavor, a unique temptation. I could sense their pulses. The rush of blood beneath their fragile skin. Tonight, my appetite would not be easily sated. It was one that demanded sustenance and the sweet surrender of flesh. A craving that would lead me to claim life after life, leaving only silence and shadows in my wake.

A sharp scent knifed through the city's tangled stench, jolting me from my thoughts with a force that had me almost flinching. Fresh blood—warm, recently spilled—and beneath it, something intoxicating yet oddly familiar. My brow furrowed, irritation flickering through my gut.

A fledgling. The realization hit me like cold water, instantly kindling my irritation into seething annoyance. Some reckless sire had created a new vampire and let them roam with no direction, no decorum. The arrogance of such an act was staggering. New vampires were forbidden to roam unaccompanied due to their volatile nature. It was dangerous, reckless, and frankly insulting to our kind.

My teeth clenched, my grip tightening on the wheel. Tonight was supposed to be mine alone, an evening of carefully curated pleasures, not babysitting a careless whelp. I pressed the accelerator, turning a sharp right. The mustang bucked beneath me, growling its fury, as I gave chase.

The deserted streets and dim alleyways the perfect playground. As I navigated toward the origin, I glanced through each as I passed. My irritation grew with every passing moment. The infantile being was not even attempting discretion. Her scent, a beacon that pulled at the hunter in me. Such arrogance from a fledgling was intolerable.

The scent grew stronger as I neared a run down dive bar, nestled in a dilapidated part of the city. My eyes caught site of an open door halfway down a dimly lit alley. The old fluorescent street light flickered from years of neglect. The light above the door keeping time with it. Here, the fledgling's aura slammed into me. The strength of her feral hunger pulled at my own. Underneath the scent of death lingered youthful uncertainty.

I parked a block over in a residential area. Many of the streetlamps were in the same shape as the one in the alley. Boarded up houses dotted the street and the few that were inhabited were quiet given the late hour. Stepping from the car, I cut through the yards, jumping the high metal fence separating the houses from the alley. Irritation coiled tightly within me as I closed the distance. When I confronted this foolish little whelp, their death would be swift. We were meant to be legend, not scream our existence to the world.

I approached the open door that lay just inside the entrance from the alley. The scene that greeted me was one for the books. A mortal lay dead at her feet, blood pooling richly beneath him. She was crouched like a predator ready to strike. Blood smeared across her lips. Her features a mixture of horror and exhilaration. She was little more than a child in this existence. And she dared to hunt in the open and dangerously close to mortal discovery.

I stared at her as I smelled myself mingled with her scent. It was obvious I was her sire. I shook my head with disbelief and shock. Frustration burned at my own carelessness. Recognition slammed into me with a brutal force. She was the woman from that night…from the car accident. I took a deep breath and another smell, faint and weak, drifted through. This one was older, familiar…ancient. The knowingness of it pulled at memories long since locked away.

She growled low in her throat, eyes narrowed with warning, failing to recognize who was standing before her. Her pupils dilated in fear, swallowing the irises with them. Her nostrils flared as she took a deep breath through her nose, getting the full force of my scent. I watched her eyes go wide with recognition of me, as her sire. Good, I thought coldly; she was at least smart enough to sense her mistake.

I felt a sense of reluctant pride at her boldness, yet it was tempered by my dismay at the inconvenience of having to care for this grown child.

"Do you have any idea the trouble your recklessness could have caused? Do you not understand…we do not kill openly, nor do we kill certain prey?" I could not hide the growing rage in my voice.

She backed up slightly, uncertainty overtaking her prior defiant stance. Her eyes widened and darted around the dilapidated office space. The ceiling and walls were splattered with the vestiges of her meal's life force. Guilt and doubt peeked through before her gaze landed back on me. Then, they pinched taking me in, assessing me, sizing me up.

Her expression shifted as she began to recognize me through our bond. Her posture shifting from a rabid animal ready to attack, to one of submission. Good, I thought darkly; she was finally understanding the gravity of her situation.

Chapter 3

Kallea

I licked my fingers as I relished the final traces of the young bartender. His taste lingered like ripe fruit—sweet, strong, untouched by age or bitterness. His blood had been untainted by alcohol or drugs. Clean and pure…a rare delicacy. Hazel eyes stared upward. Mouth frozen open in an unanswered, desperate prayer. I inhaled deeply, smelling death and the beginnings of decay…and something else.

Something ancient.

Primeval and dark.

My mind struggled, refusing to define whatever approached. The shift in the air abrupt. It thickened into an oppressive weight, choked by a scent alien to this century or any other. It felt as if time itself had forged this presence from darkness, iron, and unrelenting evil.

My muscles tightened and my senses went on alert. I dropped low, fingers pressed against the matted carpet, coiled and ready to strike. As the unidentified smell crept closer, no footsteps or breath disrupted the stillness of the room. It screamed its dominance with no tangible presence and under it all, lay the twinge of deja vu.

Laughter…low and menacing…slithered down the hallway, coiling itself around me, pushing me off balance. Hatred surged in me, even without knowing the source. Its very presence brought my hackles to rise and the fight in me to increase. I was a predator and I was not about to let some unseen force have power over me.

He stepped into view, filling the doorway. Broad shoulders strained against a thin white tank, muscles carved like marble beneath dark jeans. But it wasn't his imposing physique that held me captive—it was his eyes.

Liquid amber fixed on me with condescension and dominance. If the eyes are the windows to the soul, then the man in front of me was absent one. His arrogance evident in the way he leaned against the doorjamb.

I growled—a savage warning laced within it. The primal part of my brain unable to fully grasp what or who stood before me. The only thing I could ascertain was that it was dangerous. He laughed again. The sound was deep and hollow, laced with mockery. It set my teeth on edge and ignited my irritation. Just as I prepared to lunge, he spoke, shattering my instincts and forcing my mind to clear.

"Do you have any idea the trouble your recklessness could have caused? Do you not understand…we do not kill openly, nor do we kill certain prey?" I winced at the tone of his voice and felt myself unwind, withdrawing from his orbit slightly.

I saw his eyes roam around the room, landing on the man—dead— next to me. A low growl vibrated in my throat, quickly dying when I realized there was something unearthly familiar about him. As he took a step closer, I hunched myself tighter. Muscles aching and ready to launch at him.

"Come now, pet," he purred. Voice rich with sinister amusement. "I have no interest in your stale little snack. Its usefulness has…expired."

Words eluded me. My mind was clouded by raw, animalistic need as it fought with confusion and fear. I remained crouched, wary as he approached. That smile, a cold mask that never reached those wicked eyes—deepened slightly.

"Apparently, I was careless in leaving you behind," he murmured. "But perhaps fate intervened. You may yet serve a purpose greater than mere survival. I can always use a companion to 'warm' me on colder nights."

He advanced further, with the confidence of an immortal life. "I have existed far longer than your feeble mind can fathom. I have witnessed humanity's fall from grace to gutter. I'll tame you or kill you. That choice, my pet, is yours alone. Though, I must warn you, I do not like having to put down my pets."

He extended a hand—strong, elegant, radiating power and ancient authority. I snapped at the offered appendage and scooted back further. He was in my space and I wanted him to leave. I did not want to go with him, at the same time I did. The vacillation kept me on edge, an ache crept in behind my eyes. Did vampires get headaches?

He lowered his hand. The look on his face communicated his displeasure and it rippled through me. I shuddered, drawing deeper into myself. He crouched in front of me until we were almost nose to nose. Centuries of age danced within his oppressive gaze and it pulled at me.

"Who?" I croaked, barely audible. My mind wavered in and out of rational thought. I did not trust him and yet part of me was drawn to him. It was as if an invisible thread pulled me to him.

His smile widened slightly. Offered no warmth. Only a clear assertion of his strength. His body vibrated with an ancient knowing. A presence that was more than mere flesh and bone. It was as if he was forged from history, raised in shadow, and flourished in the dark. Nothing about him suggested safety. Carelessness around him would lead to death.

"Who I am will become clear soon enough. For now, my name is Vakor. I will help you understand whose blood now flows through your veins. Who you are supposed to be."

I took his hand and rose with him. Doubt still plagued my mind and I wanted to run, yet I knew I had to go with him. Guilt roared through me like a category 5 hurricane. I hated taking life. Each kill awakened something disturbingly erotic within me. My thighs dampened, betraying my arousal.

We moved through the darkness—heavy yet, light as a whisper on the wind, disconnected from the world around us. Everything felt surreal…fragmented. The shadows flowed beside me as though they were sentient beings obediently accompanying their pied piper.

The alleyway twisted and turned, a maze of trash-strewn paths and crumbling brick walls. Each step resonated through me. Amplifying not only the sensation of my own feet on cold pavement but also the pulse of life hidden within the city's veins.

This heightened awareness remained overwhelming. Whispered conversations behind walls. Stray animals scavenged through garbage. The steady heartbeats of mortals as they slept, oblivious to the darkness prowling nearby.

He guided me along the alley, headed toward an unknown destination. His presence overpowered me leaving me feeling claustrophobic. Fingers gripped mine tight as we walked to an unknown destination. Every instinct screamed to flee from the suffocating hold he had on me. Yet, something deeper, twisted and newly awakened, kept me at his side—submissive and inexplicably compliant.

"Where are we going?" My voice trembled.

The man in front of me gave off no illusions of prior humanity. His movements were too fluid. His demeanor too arrogant. Everything about him screamed, "otherworldly" and deadly. I could not stop the internal tug-of-war between wanting to go with him and wanting to run. The way he held and pulled me only concreted his threat from earlier. Submit or die.

"We're getting you cleaned up," he answered. The casual tone made it seem as though this were an everyday occurrence. "Fresh clothes from your place, then to mine. Your true education begins tonight."

"My place?" My panic surged pushing me into flight mode. "No… Anthony—he'll freak out, call the cops…or worse, try to kill us."

I struggled to pull my hand from his as we emerged from the alley. He led me through long forgotten lawns then down a deserted side street, and away from prying eyes. We stopped at his vehicle, where his hand moved from mine up to my bicep. His grip harder than previous with a look that demanded obedience. The sleek muscle car matched him in power and darkness.

"My dear sweet pet," he laughed. His voice dripped mockery, "no mortal—or immortal—can kill us. You will learn the myths of the vampire, are just that: myths. It is insulting. Yet, our depravity and ruthlessness are underplayed truths."

His words cascaded through my bones like a death knell. The truth hit hard—too swift, too certain. It coiled in my gut with a weight I could not yet identify. I believed him, though part of me wished I didn't. The way the night embraced him, as though he were a familiar friend. His confidence flowed off of him, presenting the illusion of aloofness, hiding the danger within.

"How do you know where I live?" I whispered, dread clawing deeper into my chest.

He chuckled. "What do you think?"

"If I knew the answer, I wouldn't have asked the question. Can you just answer a question without deflecting or asking one in return?"

Dread may have clawed into my chest, yet his flippancy ignited nothing but rage and irritation.

This vacillation between my humanity and the wanna be predator I was grated on my nerves, just as much as he did, and I had only just met him. Yet, the truth of his claim of being my sire, tugged at the edge of my consciousness.

This time, his smile fully reached his eyes—devoid of joy, filled instead with control and challenge. He was nothing like the legends of books or screen—he was something far more dangerous and compelling. This alone piqued my curiosity, keeping me at his side.

"Pet, while I do appreciate your inquisitive nature," he said. The veil of patience lifted from his tone, "it is beginning to grate on my nerves. Answers will come once you're not playing tug-of-war with your lingering mortal mind."

His gaze narrowed, irritation and amusement blending. "We'll get your clothing, and once cleaned up, I'll answer your questions. Until then, Shut. The. Fuck. Up. And. Get. In."

The final words fell out of his mouth with a pointed silkiness, leaving no room for argument. I swallowed, lowering myself into his car and settling into the warm leather seats. The interior of the car smelled like cedar and sandalwood. Such an odd combination for someone like him. His old scent mixed in there too.

The angrier I became, the more the predator in me fought to come out and take control again. I struggled with this internal war so much throughout the past…whoever knows how long…and no matter what I did, I could not silence it.

There was also this creeping feeling that something lurked inside of me, something deep within the deepest recess of my mind, my soul, that wanted out but could not figure out how to break free. The shadows pulsated and moved throughout the dark interior of the car.

"Mistress come to us…"

"Break free from her."

"She is nothing."

"She is mistress."

"He will save her"

"He will bring her"

"AAAAaaa shut up…shut up…get the fuck out of my head." I screamed at nothing and everything. I gripped my hands over my ears, praying for the onslaught of voices to go away.

He looked at me quizzically. "Please tell me you are not one of those humans who have mental issues."

"No." My teeth clenched as the whispers continued unbothered by my hands over my ears. They rattled around inside my skull leaving me feeling bruised. "Since you did this to me. I can hear whispering everywhere. They keep repeating 'Mistress'."

"You can hear the shadows?" His eyes were wide with disbelief and confusion.

"Hear the shadows? I hear strange voices in my head that make me feel like I am going insane. The incessant whispering feels like love and hate burning and stabbing my brain. I hate it. I want it to stop." I couldn't hide the turmoil any longer. I did not want to, not for this frightening male next to me, even though my blood hummed and pulled me to him, and not for my own chaotic mind.

"Interesting. Shadows do not speak to those created. Only to those born in the shadow. A unique gift, indeed. One that we will have to explore after we finish with our task."

His words unsettled me more than they offered comfort. As much as I wanted to inquire what he meant by that statement, the energy to form the question was not there. I curled myself further into the seat, allowing the purr of the engine, the vibrations of the vehicle, and the noise of the tires to lull me into a fragile calm.

I could not understand how I had been so blind and naive to the reality of the night. Nothing made sense anymore. Up was down, left was right, and fucked up was normal…or whatever cliche statement you wanted to use to describe this current…whatever the hell it is, then by all means, someone better.

Chapter 4

Kallea

I gripped the door handle so tightly my knuckles ached. My skin strained against bone, white over tense tendons. Streetlights and neon smeared past the glass, colors bled together until my eyes watered. My chest rose too fast, dragging in air that scraped down my throat like razors.

The world beyond the car was irrelevant now to me. A mocking blur of human life. Why should it matter? This city wasn't mine anymore. It belonged to them. Not to things like me. Not to the ones who fed and killed without a second thought. And yet… I thought. I wanted to stop. I couldn't stop and that was my curse.

Something lived inside me, an intruder that had worn my skin long enough to think it owned me. It slid through my veins like heat, curling up my spine, pressing against the base of my skull. My teeth ached. I wanted to tell myself I was still in control, that the thing inside me was nothing more than instinct.

But it had a rhythm all its own, and I could feel my heart syncing to it. My pulse wasn't mine anymore. It built, and with each beat the world sharpened. The tap of shoes on pavement outside, the quick gasp of someone laughing down the street.

The whispers grew louder, pressing at the edges of my skull until I thought my teeth might crack from clenching them. *Closer. Tear. Take.* My fingers flexed on the handle, trying to push the whispers into it and out of my head. The leather of the door panel cool against my fingers and a stark contrast to the textured plastic of the handle. Every feed the whispers grew more incessant and it was exhausting.

Was my mind cracked open like a busted watermelon? Or had becoming a vampire stripped away the humanity that once kept me sane? Was this some twisted gift—a clairvoyance of predators?

Not fucking likely. Gifts didn't make you want to murder the first warm body you smelled. Nothing made sense to me and the more I tried to unravel it, the more I struggled. Every answer led to more questions, which led to more heartache.

God, I sounded ridiculous. Like a child imagining they might wake up with superpowers. I wasn't a hero. Not even the dark, broken kind. I was a monster. A monster with something inside her that wanted nothing but to drown the world in blood and chaos.

And the worst part? Some part of me wanted it too. A part of me purred at the idea of letting the homicidal maniac inside out. The voices even wanted it released…so why was I fighting it?

The glass between me and the street caught my reflection. My eyes were darker than they should be, pupils swallowing color. My lips pulled back in a grimace. The pressure in my head increased with an urgency I could not place.

The car slowed, turning into streets I used to know. Old brick dressed up to look new, LED strips humming against the night. Once I'd walked here without thinking. Now, I was the reason the streets were not safe anymore. It was the ultimate millennial and Gen Z location with its ecofriendly, trend setting living spaces and shops.

It all seemed ridiculous now. We lived here because it was the "cool" thing to do, yet it also meant we were working to live instead of living and working. The nouveau riche aesthetic being the biggest attraction.

He parked outside my building. Recognition hit like ice water over fire. Behind those walls had been warmth, laughter, and love. The life of a woman who had the world at her finger tips. My shoulders hunched and my breath went jagged. I couldn't go in there. Not like this…I didn't want to kill Anthony.

"Come, pet," he murmured, voice smooth as fabric over a blade. "I have the perfect remedy for your hunger."

"How will this help?" The words were thin, breaking apart before they were fully formed. Warm scent drifted from somewhere above— salt, alcohol, something sweet—and the ache inside me flared. My nails scraped the leather beside me, tearing a thin line in the seat.

"Control yourself," he said. The calm in his voice, worse than anger. "Let will and instinct work together. Lose the balance, and you are a liability. I do not tolerate liabilities."

The word *control* grated down my spine. My tongue pressed against the tips of my teeth, tasting the air. I could hear them now— the uneven thump of human hearts, the hushed murmurs of life behind the industrial walls. I knew in the midst of it all was the man I loved. The man I was supposed to marry. I wonder if he worried about me.

He smiled, and it was all bone under skin, cold and precise. Again, the desire to bolt spiked in me, yet here I stayed next to him.

"Those violet eyes," he murmured. Gaze tracing me like a blade. His finger holding my chin up to level us eye to eye. "Rare. Enticing. A stunning flaw. Do not make me regret my mercy, pet."

He moved with that lethal ease, rounding to my side and opening the door. His hand reached for me, inviting and threatening all the same. My head snapped forward before I knew it, teeth closing on empty air.

His laugh was low, curling into the space between us. Then his fingers closed around my arm, pain biting deep. My knees bent to resist, but the heat inside me surged, turning the pain into something hotter. I scolded myself in my head at my unhealthy reaction to him.

The building's doors gave way to the cool scent of stone and steel. My breath came faster with every step we took. Somewhere above, music pulsed, heavy with bass, laughter weaving through it. And under it all—the warm, rich throb of life.

The elevator's gate groaned shut. I could feel the walls around us, smell the dust in the metal. His eyes stayed on me as I hunched to the floor, but I barely noticed. My focus pointed at the floors above. To the air that seeped through the cracks. To the heartbeats that skipped every third beat like a stuttered invitation.

By the time we reached the fifth floor, my fingers were trembling. Not from fear, but anticipation.

—VAKOR—

She crouched in the corner, knees drawn up, body angled away as though she was making herself smaller. Dirt and blood mapped pale skin, streaking across delicate cheekbones. Crimson hair clung in tangled knots against her head. Beneath the filth, muscle lay taut and ready, every line carved by instinct.

Her eyes found mine, and a thread pulled tight in my chest. Not recognition—something older, buried deep enough its shape blurred when I tried to see it. The bond between us whispered faintly, a flicker of her resistance pressing against me and then fading.

I remembered the first taste of her. Even then, there had been a note that didn't belong. A flavor that curled at the edge of my memory. Now it slid just out of reach, like a name I couldn't recall. I kept my distance. The urge to taste her again was too sharp, and she would fight hard enough to make a mess.

"Where have you been staying?" The words left me without warmth.

Her glare cut back and her brows furrowed, answering without sound. Nowhere. Everywhere. Her edges had been stripped clean of the human veneer, leaving raw instinct beneath. She would be beautiful once washed, but beauty was the least dangerous thing about her. The others would see there was something otherworldly about her, and that sparked a note of something in me.

The elevator jolted, its steel ribs shuddering. She shifted closer, not in trust, but in readiness, weight shifting over the balls of her feet. A different pull rose in me at her closeness, quick and unwelcome, like a nerve struck wrong. My jaw tightened as I raked my fingers through my hair. Was I becoming possessive of her?

What was she?

Why did the air between us hum with familiarity I couldn't place?

I reached inward for the thread she had stirred. My own mind recoiled with a lance of pain, forcing a wince to cross my face. Whatever waited there was not meant to be touched—not yet. I let it go and stepped into the hall.

The corridor to 5B was all polished brick and clean lines. The air humming faintly with the sounds of the humans going about their lives. Gold fixtures gleamed against the dark paint. A careful attempt at modern luxury, when it was nothing more than lipstick on a pig. I caught the layered scent ahead—liquor, perfume, sweat—and beneath it, the sweet heat of blood moving under skin.

I knocked once. The sharp rap of my knuckles echoed down the still hallway. Anticipation curled through me as my fangs slid down. I glanced at her, the feral shine in her eyes answering mine.

"Now, my pet… your training begins."

A voice floated from inside, light and careless. "Just a sec!"

I heard light footsteps dancing toward us. The door opened on a woman with dark hair, laughter still on her mouth.

"Hey, can I help you?" she asked.

"Not me…her"

I stepped aside, revealing my pet, crouched down behind me.

The woman's eyes widened, amusement freezing. Her breath caught—once, twice—before her voice broke.

"…Kallea?"

Chapter 5

Kallea

"…Kallea?"

Her voice shattered the silence, fragile and trembling with disbelief. My name—a ghostly echo from a past life—hung in the air before my sire violently shoved her back into the apartment.

Her dark hair whipped around her pale face, blue eyes wide with shock. Only when I registered the stark panic on her face did I realize I was growling.

Pure, primal dread surged from her. Her heart pounded, a frantic rhythm thrumming deliciously in my ears. Each beat quickened my hunger, feeding something monstrous deep within me. Shame washed through me, hot and bitter, yet I couldn't deny the twisted pleasure her terror evoked.

My sire's chuckle reverberated through the room—as he strolled toward the whiskey bottle on the counter, like he lived here. The amber liquid glinted dully under dim lights as he poured it. This simple action cementing his presence in the space.

From deeper within the apartment, above the relentless thump of music, a familiar voice sliced through my thoughts. "Kallea? We haven't received new information about her. We've been worried. It's so unlike her to just vanish. They found her car and a body inside. But she's gone…"

Anthony.

His voice struck me like a physical blow—sharp, painful, tearing open wounds I thought were sealed. My eyes widened as footsteps approached from the narrow hallway. Heavy. Precise. Purposeful.

The woman who'd answered the door was now pressed desperately against the wall, frozen, as if wishing to dissolve into the peeling paint. Her breath came in tiny, panicked whimpers. Each small gasp pulled at the monstrous hunger building within me. My fight to control it becoming harder the longer we stood there. She kept glancing at the hallway, mouth opening and closing as though deciding to scream or not.

"Shhhh… we wouldn't want to make this more than it has to be." Vakor's voice drifted past me and I watched the woman stiffen.

Anthony spoke again from the back room—fast, clipped, detached. His voice had the business tone he reserved for dismissing unwanted clients or unprofitable meetings. It was what made him a valuable player in the marketing industry. He could sell anything to anyone and he could shut them down just as easily.

"James, everything needs to be wrapped by Monday. No one's heard from Kallea in nearly a year. I can't keep sitting on the revenue. Cancel all of it. The venue. The caterer. The DJ. Everything that was tied to her. Yes, James. I mean it. I need to move on."

Cancel me.

Move on.

I staggered back, every muscle tense, knees nearly buckling beneath the crushing weight of memories and betrayal. My vision blurred at the edges as dread pooled hot and heavy in my stomach. I couldn't breathe or speak—trapped, rooted in place as Anthony stepped into view.

Was I that easy to move on from?

Was I that forgettable?

Had he ever loved me?

"Kallea…it is me. Amber. Remember? I am your best friend." Her voice wavered, unshed tears brimming in her eyes.

"Amber" Her name tasted rancid in my mouth. I knew she spoke the truth, yet under it a lie clung, like a tick.

I brushed my fingers down her cheek, twirling a section of her hair in my fingers. She smelled like lemon and honey. A strange combination of sweet and sour. Every fiber of my being screamed at me. There was something I am missing, something my internal voice was trying to get me to look at.

"What happened to you? Where have you been?" She peppered me with questions. Most of them falling before they reached my ears.

—VAKOR—

The man's voice—sharp, calculating, and utterly ignorant of the doom approaching him—preceded him into the room. He ended his call abruptly, leaving the faint, lingering echo behind.

Anthony. The fiancé. Arrogant in his belief that the inconvenient messiness of death could be erased by simply 'unloading' revenue. The human male made my hackles raise. He may be human, yet I could sense the taint of evil in him. His detachment when talking about Kallea grated at me.

He appeared at last, confident expression rapidly dissolving into confusion and alarm. His gaze darted frantically from the trembling, feral form of Kallea to the terrified woman pressed against the wall, finally landing on me—composed and unruffled. A predator savoring the chaos.

"Anthony," I drawled. His name bitter, yet satisfying, like well-aged poison, on my tongue. "It seems we've interrupted your festivities. Do you have room for two more?"

My voice wrapped around him like an inevitable fate. each flicker of horror surfacing clearly in his features. I watched intently as comprehension shattered his careful composure. His eyes widened, disbelief and panic warring openly in his expression. Tonight, his comfortable, ordered world would crumble, and I intended to enjoy every exquisite moment of it.

"Who are you and why are you here? His tone was clipped and a little too confident for his fragility.

I met his question with a laugh. The sound of it was a seismic vibration that rattled the glasses next to me. I sized up the male standing in front of me. He appeared well muscled under the baggy t-shirt and sweatpants, and his pulse strong. By all intents and purposes he was a healthy specimen. And that is where my admiration ended.

He was nothing more than sustenance for my kind. No amount of strength would lend a saving hand for him. I could see his posture shifting into a defensive stance as he found his bravery. My amusement amping up at the sight.

I rolled my eyes. "Oh puhlease…do stop the chest puffing. You inconsequential pest." I said. "Who I am is none of your concern and what I am doing here is not about me. It is about her."

I pointed to Kallea, who appeared oblivious to our exchange as she was too caught up with the human female. Her movements more fluid than when I first found her huddled over that corpse. The savage within her tempered slightly. Anthony followed my finger to stare at her.

Recognition wavered in his eyes. Disbelief peaking through before I saw the brief flash of fury then fear. He thought she was gone because of the poison in her veins that night when I first found her. The night she was turned unbeknownst to me.

"She's alive?" A barely registered question slipped from his lips. Shock settled firmly into place.

He turned toward her, taking slow steps. The closer he got to her, the more I could see her muscles rippling as she became more aware of his creeping presence. I was half tempted to let her attack him if he touched her. Though allowing that to happen would mean another blood bath to clean and cover up.

"I would not get too close to her. You may not like what happens." I could not hide the encouragement laced within those words. I mean, why would I actually warn him?

I knew he would not listen and at this point, I needed some entertainment. Anything to turn the tide of this night. I had not planned on finding a whelp…and not just any whelp…MY progeny. The power radiating under her skin kept me invested in her success. She was different and I still had not worked out what it was about her.

"Anthony. Help." I heard the squeak from the human woman as Kallea leaned in to sniff her.

The bloodlust amplified the longer she stood there. It was affecting me as well. After all, we sensed every change within the human body as a way to keep us from consuming spoiled blood. It did not hurt us. It just did not provide any satiation and could cause blood rage in fledglings.

"Amber…Are you okay? Have they hurt you?"

How cute. He cared for the pathetic girl.

"It's Kallea. She is acting weird." This time the tears began to flow down her face.

Oh this is indeed going to be fun.

Chapter 6
Unknown

I marveled—genuinely marveled—at the pitiful grandeur these creatures had crafted with their fragile hands and feeble minds. Towers clawed arrogantly at the heavens; roads stretched out paved in hardened black stone; machines roared like untamed beasts, crawling endlessly like blind insects. Their sprawling cities pulsed with countless artificial suns, thrusting defiantly into the night, crafting a feeble illusion of safety. A neon-lit deception they desperately clung to.

They believed their precious lights could shield them, holding the darkness at bay. As though I couldn't glide effortlessly through their blinding fluorescents and harsh LEDs, as easily as I once walked among the stars themselves.

Pathetic.

Two flawless beings, crafted from pure divine essence, had once carried the breath of holiness itself. And from that perfection had come… this. A swarm of hollow, diseased, self-absorbed beings convinced their glass towers elevated them to godhood. No trace of their divine origin remained—only filth, noise, and ceaseless frantic motion. Forever fleeing, eternally terrified, oblivious to how their lives hung by a thread, fragile as tissue paper.

They disgusted me.

The vaunted compassion of their Creator, His so-called infinite mercy, was nowhere to be found. Instead, deviance skittered openly through shadowed alleys and beneath glaring streetlights alike. Humanity scrambled blindly from one meaningless point to another, forgetting entirely that their existence was built on emptiness, held together by illusions ready to crumble at the slightest misstep.

They forgot their origins.

But I hadn't.

I remembered Adam. I remembered Lilith.

I remembered exactly how it began.

When the Creator shaped Adam and Lilith, He embedded each with a spark—a fragment of angelic essence. A critical, fatal flaw. Lilith, like all females crafted after heaven's fierce image, was dominant, lethal, brilliant. Adam was softer, malleable, and dangerously curious. Precisely what had intrigued Lucifer—not from love, but from a twisted, cynical fascination.

God couldn't bear it.

Lilith was banished. Thrown from Eden into purgatory. The meticulously crafted oubliette just for her. A dark and empty cage to trap a woman He couldn't control. Then came Eve—a submissive doll, hollow and obedient.

Lucifer, ever defiant, rebelled violently. His spite ignited Hell's eternal fires. Every moment since had been an elaborate, endless retaliation. A bitter, mocking defiance of the divine Father. A middle finger thrown at him.

I chuckled, the sound dark and resonant, memories blossoming like poisoned flowers in my mind. Even now, recalling all the Master had lost filled me with savage pleasure. So much fury, so much arrogance— wasted upon two fragile creatures of clay daring to defy their Creator.

Humanity had always been doomed.

The instant Eve's teeth pierced the apple's skin, their fate sealed—humanity condemned. Yet still, these pathetic creatures raced frantically from the flames licking their souls, unaware they burned already, from within.

I had waited—endured thousands of silent, shadow-bound years, watching from the darkness.

My moment had finally arrived, ripe with vengeance and long-awaited retribution.

Chapter 7

Kallea

"Kallea… you're alive."

Anthony's voice was sharp against my ears. His words dripped with malice and forced surprise. A poorly executed performance as his phone clattered to the floor. He moved toward me in a clumsy rush, desperation staining the air.

His hand reached for my shoulder, and the stench of his guilt— anger, confusion, resentment—washed over me, thick and suffocating. My body recoiled instinctively; a low growl erupted from deep within my chest, responding to the vile touch of his fingers. I snapped at his fingers, nipping one at his delayed withdrawal.

A singular drop of blood welled on the tip of his finger. I bared my fangs in response to the smell and went to lunge at him. Fully intending to rip his throat out. Another hand, firmer this time, touched my shoulder, pushing me back, holding me in place. I growled and swiped at Anthony while snapping at the hand on me.

"My pet," Vakor's smooth voice poked at me. "Remember who you are. A glorious creature, not a wild beast."

His words sliced through the fog clouding my mind, anchoring me firmly to reality. I looked toward him—this being who had forged me into something monstrous yet undeniably powerful. There was no humanity behind those amber eyes, only ancient cruelty, unfeeling and calculating. His smile held no warmth, merely an expression of dominance.

My senses sharpened as the hunger in me grew painful and violent in its need to be satiated. I felt the heartbeat of the room—the frantic pulse of Anthony, the trembling fear radiating from Amber. Her delicate body pressed tightly against the wall. Her whimpers teased my beast and called to me. Her fragrance sweet and sour, tinged with anxiety. Each small, rapid breath stirring the frenzy rapidly building in me.

Anthony tormented me further by standing rigidly still. His body covered in bulky clothing did not hide the reality that I knew every inch of it intimately. His fear blended with his fury—an irresistible combination pulling at my primal instincts. I wanted him—wanted to taste the strength of his blood, feel it surge warm and vibrant down my throat.

"What… have… you… done… to… her?" he demanded, each word bitten off with hateful precision.

Vakor's laughter filled the room, a cruel, hollow sound. "Me? I merely gave her a gift beyond your comprehension. A life that transcends your petty attempts to end hers. You filled her veins with poison, hoping she'd quietly fade away. I filled her with something far greater—strength and unending life."

Rage flashed hot across Anthony's face, overtaking his fear. He lunged forward, fists balled, teeth bared.

"I do not know what you are talking about. Who the fuck are you?" The vehemence of his words should have lent to their truthfulness. Instead, they belied that he had no remorse for what he did to me. "She is my fiancé. We were to be married when she vanished."

In a blur of motion, Vakor's hand shot out, clamping firmly around Anthony's throat and lifting him off his feet. Anthony's face reddened from the lack of air. Legs kicked weakly. Fingers clawed uselessly at the iron grip holding him aloft.

"So strong yet utterly useless," Vakor mocked, in that chilling calm he did so well. "Perhaps you envy me and wish to taste what real power is, for yourself? But forgive my manners."

I watched Anthony lower to the floor, the grip around his neck loosening. Vakor traced a single razor-sharp claw along his jaw, drawing blood with horrifying precision.

"A reminder, Anthony," he whispered. "Now, sit quietly and behave." His tongue danced along the cut, tasting his essence.He spat after a moment, wincing as though the blood was bad.

Anthony's eyes glazed over, mind succumbing without resistance. His movement mechanical as he walked to the old, battered couch—my couch, our couch, and sat blankly, awaiting commands that would come.

Vakor walked toward Amber and me, her sobs quiet yet frantic. Anger surged as I inhaled her. There amongst the citrus was him. Their betrayal wafted around her. My humanity cracked at the weight of this revelation. My supposed best friend sleeping with my fiancé, as though I did not matter to either of them.

"She reeks of you," I spat at Anthony, rage bubbling over. "Was she your comfort while I rotted? Your solace after poisoning me? Did her sweet cunt give you the attention you so desperately craved?"

My scream was feral, untamed, as I lunged forward. Vakor's hand seized my shoulder. His grip bruising, holding me with little effort. I wanted to rip her throat out while Anthony watched his fuck toy die before I took his too.

"Gentle, my pet," he warned, voice low, dangerously soft. "Control is key. Just a gentle bite, off to the side. Don't kill—savor."

His instructions pulled my wrath into a razor-edged focus. My fangs emerged smoothly as I leaned in, gently piercing Amber's neck. Blood flowed, hot and rich, a deep metallic nectar flooding my mouth. Warmth bloomed within me, intoxicating and empowering, every nerve ending ignited with euphoria.

"Enough, now," Vakor commanded softly. "Leave her dazed, confused, obedient."

He turned Amber toward him, his voice a silken spell: "You saw nothing. You drank too much. You feel sick. You need sleep. Go now."

She obeyed instantly, disappearing down the hallway—toward my room, my bed, my stolen life.

Hatred exploded anew within me, cold and deadly. She lay where I'd once dreamed, where Anthony had whispered empty promises. I trembled violently, restraint fraying at the edges of my mind.

"Why Anthony? How long?" I winced inwardly at the pleading and pathetic tone of my voice. Vakor was the embodiment of death and composure. Then there was me…whiny and weak. "Did I mean nothing to you?"

Anthony's gaze landed on me. The tight restraint of Vakor's command held him. His eyes pleaded with me, and it felt dead to me. I could not give him any grace. I would not give him compassion. I wanted answers and I was not getting them because Vakor silenced him.

I turned my angry gaze toward Vakor, tasting the lingering blood on my lips. They had stolen from me, betrayed me, attempted to erase me. "Let him speak. He owes me answers. Maybe he will give them to me, unlike you."

"You wound me little whelp." How did he find that funny? I hated this man. "Speak to her Anthony. Speak only truth. Every lie that leaves your lips will cause you to bleed at her hand."

I watched as Anthony flexed his jaw. He actually had the audacity to be pissed off. This pulled a laugh from me, one that felt unnatural. Deeper, darker, more than what should have left my throat. I felt the presence in me stirring and the whispers came through like static.

"Answer me Anthony. Tell me why." I demanded.

"You were a way in. Your father had money and connections. I wanted it." The deadpan tone of his voice was all I needed to know he spoke the truth. I took a step closer to him, just close enough to keep his words true.

"And…"

"Amber and I just happened." The hesitation in those words was a lie. I don't know how I was able to tell, but the taste of it was acrid.

I pierced his arm with my nails, pulling him to me, blood welling around their tips. "Do. Not. Lie. To. Me." I pulled my hand back, licking the blood off them. It tasted of ash and rot. I spit it on the floor before I could swallow.

"Fine. We have been together for 4 years now. Our plan was for us to marry then you were to disappear. I would get everything since your gracious father loved me so much that he did not demand a prenup." Truth. A very ugly and concrete truth.

"Money. It was about the money. He would have paid you to fuck off if that is what you wanted. Why not try to kill me sooner?" My mind spiralled at the revelation. How did I not see this asshole for who he really was?

"The night of the dinner. When we were getting ready to go. I received a call from Amber. Your father was going to break off the engagement and was taking you back to Romania after the gala. I was not about to let you go. I loved you even being with Amber too."

Truth.

Lie.

The sound of my hand crashing against his face echoed through the little living room. The sting of it filled the nerves in my hand. I licked the blood that dotted it from the cut. The side of his face turned purple, almost instantly from the force. Instant regret flared at the spoiled taste, only this time I swallowed and the whispers purred.

I stepped back from him. Shock radiated through me at him. I was nothing more than a means to wealth. Wealth my father would have showered him with if he had just asked…fuck demanded for my life. Instead he plotted to kill me and run off with that whore of Babylon. She fucked anyone. Matter of fact, I was sure she was sleeping with a husband and wife who had a few…darker kinks.

"He is yours. I will kill him if I get any closer." I told Vakor, walking to the counter and pouring myself three fingers of whiskey.

Their time would come soon enough. I would ensure it—painfully, meticulously.
With every last drop of their blood…

Chapter 8

Kallea

I looked toward the hallway where Amber disappeared. Panic quickly started to rise even as exhaustion pulled at me. The static in my head amplified even as I fought to keep it quiet. I turned to Vakor. He was watching me, one eyebrow raised, a smirk drawn across his face.

"Won't she see the bite marks in the morning and know what happened?"

The question escaped me. I was deflated from the words spoken by Anthony. My voice brittle and small. Even as the words left my lips, they felt absurd. My mind twisted chaotically, spinning from the hunger and confusion. Panic and heartbreak twisted together beneath my skin. Threatening to consume what remained of my sanity.

"No, my pet," Vakor responded. "Our saliva closes the wounds by dawn. She'll wake with nothing but vague shame and a lingering headache. Like a cheap date after too many drinks."

The stark finality of his words silenced my protest. My gaze shifted to Anthony, seated stiffly on the couch. His muscles coiled tightly, eyes blazing fiercely with a mix of terror and rage. His pulse throbbed visibly at his throat, fear blending enticingly with his anger, stoking the embers of my hunger.

"What now?" I whispered, hollow with defeat, human fragility still desperately clinging to me.

Vakor's grin widened maliciously. Eyes glittering with cruel delight. "Now, pet, we uncover the secrets hidden in this foul blood bag's mind. I've yet to feed, and he promises to be delightfully entertaining."

His guttural laughter reverberated through the apartment, shaking my already fragmented thoughts. Anthony rose mechanically, muscles twitching erratically, eyes wide and confused. His mouth opened silently—no sound escaped. He moved like a puppet bound by unseen strings.

"How?" I managed, entranced and horrified. "You didn't bite him…"

"The older we get, the stronger our ability to manipulate and control works." He stated casually, as if this was something everyone knew. "Canaanites are the only ones with this ability as we are tied to blood."

The realization turned my stomach, head spinning with disorientation. Reality fractured around me, memories slipping through my fingers like water. The metallic taste of blood clung to my tongue, nauseating me. My hair felt heavy, matted with dirt and gore. My clothing—once mine, once pristine. Now stiff with filth and dried blood.

Vakor's gaze settled on me, cold and knowing, reading my despair. "Good, my pet. You're finally regaining clarity. I feared I might need to put you down."

"Quit threatening to put me down. Fuck you. This is your fault. I am not going to be treated like this and threatened by the likes of you. So kindly fuck off." His incessant need to use threats to manipulate me finally pushed me too far.

Yes, I was a chaotic mess.

Yes, I still clung to my humanity.

Yes, I was all over the place and irritating him was the last thing I wanted to do. And yet, as much as I feared him, I also wanted to fight against him.

"To be a threat means I would not really do it. I do not make idle threats, pet. I state facts." His words stole the air from my lungs—not from the truth behind them, but from his chilling detachment. "Allow me to feed. Interrupt again, and your end will come swiftly."

Before I could blink, Vakor seized Anthony, sinking his fangs deeply into his throat. Wet, indulgent slurping filled my ears, horrifying and captivating at the same time. Anthony's body went slack. His face morphed grotesquely into twisted pleasure. Eyes glazed and distant.

When Vakor pulled back, blood coated his lips, his expression twisted in euphoric menace. He licked them, savoring every drop, a flicker of disgust dotting his features before whispering hypnotic lies into Anthony's ear, reshaping his memories, erasing truth.

I trailed numbly behind, a ghost haunting its former life. Anthony moved silently down the familiar hall toward our room. My heart constricted as he stepped inside.

Amber lay there, curled peacefully in the bed—my bed, my sheets. Even though I heard the words leave Anthony's mouth, confirming the affair, I still did not want to believe it. I did not want to see it. Betrayal crashed over me with brutal force. My roommate. My trusted friend. Sleeping comfortably in my sheets, nestled in my stolen life.

Betrayal exploded into rage and it tore through me, raw and blinding. My fangs pushed forward, my vision tunneling as emotions boiled over. I lunged—but Vakor's grip tightened mercilessly on my shoulder, stopping me mid-motion.

"He's been with her all this time, pet," he whispered cruelly. "You've been gone for nearly a year. He never bothered searching for you—not when he had your fortune at his disposal. He told you as much."

Ice filled my veins as the truth sank in. "He has my trust. Everything my grandmother left me. He has everything that was mine. She is living my life with him."

"We will reclaim what is yours," he stated. "Leave him to rot in the filth he created. My lawyer awaits. Your affairs need settling."

With a dismissive turn, he left me standing in the wreckage of my life. I stared at Anthony's prone form beside her, his pillow stained with his own blood. Beside him—Amber. My friend turned traitor.

Vengeance surged anew, cold and calculating. I stormed into the closet, tearing through Amber's clothing, shredding silk and denim in animalistic fury. My screams—laced with hurt, anger, and despair— filled the room.

Eight years, betrayed. Eight years of loyalty shattered by greed and lust. I was a means to an end to him, nothing more, nothing less. He spewed words of love yet he stuck his dick in someone else. He claimed I was his only one, while he pined after my family's fortune. Money he did not earn. Money he would never earn because he was a lazy, arrogant twat.

It was his own fault he was only an "apprentice" at that marketing company. He was the one who kept flunking out of school. He was the one who thought he shouldn't have to work that hard because we would survive off my income and my trust fund. HE thought he should just be a trophy husband. He didn't even want me working because he felt it was beneath people like us. You know, wealthy…entitled.

Well look at him now…some trophy husband. Blood matted his face where Vakor cut him and purple bloomed where I slapped him. Then an idea struck. I walked to the bed, lifting him with ease, rolling him over to face the other direction, scrubbing the dried blood off his unmarred side. I flipped his pillow to hide the blood and moved Amber to be the little spoon.

I snatched Anthony's phone, snapping a cruel photo of their entwined betrayal. Sending it swiftly to Robin, my father's assistant, the guardian of his empire. Along with a short message that said he had been sleeping with her for years and decided he wanted to be with her. I made sure to jumble up some of it, so that it appeared like he was drunk when he sent it.

A delicious, twisted satisfaction filled me in that moment and I smiled. A genuine smile. The first in almost a year since waking up in this hell. Daddy was going to have a field day with this.

"PET. NOW."

Vakor's command shattered my murderous thoughts, forcing me to obey. I fought it. I wanted to stay and lose myself in the visions of Anthony's torture that flashed through my mind. The jumbled buzzing became clearer as I stood there.

"Yesssssssss"

"Take him"

"Feeeeeeeeeed us"

"Mistress"

"Let her out"

I turned to answer the call. My mind hazy and full of chaotic voices. I was losing my mind. As I walked away, I knew I would come for them. My anger didn't fade—it crystallized, cold and lethal. I swore Anthony would suffer as I had. He could keep my stolen life— but I would claim his soul.

Chapter 9

Kallea

When we reached the guest bathroom, Vakor had already taken it upon himself to start the shower. The steady rush of water soothed the anger still lurking within me at the thought of finally being cleansed of my disgraceful appearance.

"I found clothes for you in the closet there." Vakor said evenly. "I assumed they were yours, as they were not as…how do you say…slutty as the clothes in their room."

"You still haven't answered me," I snarled, my voice frayed at the edges. The anger coming back at the sound of his mouth making noise. "Who the fuck are you? What did you do to me?"

My words exploded forth in a desperate scream, fractured and raw. My vision flashed red, fragmented images assaulting my mind like shrapnel:

A vacant-eyed man, spikes of hair matted with blood. A drunk sprawled limply on a bench, veins grotesquely swollen, a needle dangling precariously from his pale arm. A woman shrieking, nails clawing at my face as I dragged myself into her basement—her expression frozen in endless horror, throat violently ripped open, mouth gaping silently.

All dead. All familiar. I remembered every violent detail. The sounds of their death ringing through my ears like a faint echo in the wind. I could not stop the onslaught and as it gained speed, the noise in my head grew louder. Taking deep breaths, I imagined the brick wall in my mind closing off everything. It offered me a slight reprieve, allowing me to focus every stinging emotion on the jackwagon in front of me.

"And what the fuck do you mean by 'living affairs'?" I hissed, trying to keep the desperation and rage firmly caged.

"My pet," Vakor drawled smoothly, his voice dripping with amusement, "that was more than one question."

He chuckled darkly, indifferent to the storm inside me. My fists clenched. Nails bit sharply into palms, drawing thin rivulets of blood. Yet, a different sensation arose, breaking through the red haze filling me. My body betrayed me as my thighs trembled shamefully. I squeezed them together, willing the desire to go away because he was the last person…monster I wanted to fuck.

My nipples hardened painfully beneath my shirt, the friction from my breathing sending pulses straight to my core. Slick, hot moisture gathered unbidden between my legs, fueled by lust that both disgusted and enthralled me. I couldn't help but notice the way his eyes traveled from my face to my chest.

"Hey, asshole," I growled low and feral. "My face is up here. Start fucking talking."

"Pet, you are getting a little bold now that you have fed properly." The sardonic look on his face pissed me off further even as I felt myself heating under his gaze. "I will answer your questions once we have returned to my place. It will be safer there."

"Safer. The fuck you mean safer. You are this billy badass Caananite, vampire, monster, whatever you want to fucking call yourself. How are you not safe anywhere? Unless you are all bullshit and no substance."

The look he leveled in my direction spun my mind into a whirlwind of conflicting thoughts. I wanted to fight the desire to fuck this arrogant asshole, but reason abandoned me entirely as it consumed me. I lunged, tearing at his clothing. Shredding fabric and skin alike. He matched my aggression, ripping away the last remnants of my battered clothes.

His familiarity to me felt older than time, yet I had not met him until this night. How was it I was so drawn to him? What was it about him that had me bending so freely to him even as I fought against him? The feel of his hands racing over my body, sent shivers up and down my spine. His fingers strong yet sensual in their perusal. The lingering sensation pushing me that much farther into his orbit.

The brutality of his cock slamming into me cracked the surface of the marble vanity. A scream erupted from me. Not just from the pain but also from the heightened pleasure coursing through me. His teeth sank into my nipple. The agony merged seamlessly with perverse ecstasy, spiraling directly to my core.

There was no gentleness, no pretense of affection—just brutal, primal need. Each thrust cracked the marble more beneath me. My animalistic cries bursting from my throat with every vicious thrust, carried through the apartment. It was a wonder that no one had called in a noise complaint or concerns about domestic violence.

He lifted me without breaking rhythm, pressing me hard against the shower wall. Tiles cracked behind me. Hot water cascaded over our bodies, wetting the scraps of fabric still clinging to us. None of it mattered. My body convulsed, fangs erupting through my gums, tearing through flesh in an unholy revelation of what I'd become— seeking to sink into flesh and drink the scarlet nectar just below.

Then I saw her.

Amber.

My ex-roommate, the homewrecker, pale and vulnerable. The faintest of tremors evident in her body. Her breasts brushed tantalizingly against my back as she moved behind me. Vakor's voice rasped harshly in my ear, authoritative yet mocking: "Remember… control yourself."

He released my legs, turning me forcibly to face her as she stood frozen against the shower wall. Her scent overwhelmed me, her pulse fluttering tantalizingly beneath delicate skin. Without thought, I licked, nipped, then bit deeply, my fangs sinking into the tender flesh of her breast. Her cry, a blend of fear and pleasure, ignited every nerve in me. Hot blood flooded my mouth, sending the pleasure to new heights.

Vakor's fingers gripped my hips with bone shattering force as he plunged back into my achy, needy vagina. A feral snarl tore past my lips; I wanted to destroy him, to break free. But I was still weak—too new, too raw. And let's be real, I wanted this too.

"Leave us" The words danced in a hypnotic swirl toward my former roommate. Her glassed eyes blinking, unseeing, at both of us.

Amber slipped, from the shower, without a word, dazed from compulsion. She disappeared into the shadows of the hallway, with rivulets of water tracing down her back. My anger and revulsion toward her grew, as I watched her walk away. Only to dissolve in the sudden, overwhelming pleasure building within me.

A tingling began at my toes, raced through my abdomen, igniting every nerve until a scream tore from me, shattering my consciousness in blinding release, taking the hunger and predatory rage with it.

Behind me, Vakor's body stiffened. A monstrous roar erupted from his chest, shaking through both of us as he found his release.

Then silence enveloped me, leaving only emptiness.

He withdrew, leaving me hollow as darkness rushed to claim me and dragging me down into oblivion. I barely felt the floor of the shower as I fell to greet it.

Chapter 10

Kallea

Warm… soft… safe… a beautifully crafted lie.

I clung to the darkness behind closed eyes, unwilling to abandon the fragile illusion protecting me from reality lurking just beyond consciousness. The air hung thick with unnatural fragrance, suffocating me in roses, lavender, eucalyptus, spearmint, and ylang-ylang—a sickly-sweet cocktail crafted to lull and deceive. Beneath these seductive fragrances, something darker whispered—a hint of damp decay, stagnant water, and rot that tugged insistently at my nerves.

My eyes cracked open, with reluctance, and harsh reality flooded in. Pale curtains fell like death shrouds around a towering four-poster bed. Ebony wood, dark as spilled blood, cut sharp contrasts through soft white fabric. Crimson satin sheets hissed with my every movement. They wrapped around me like a lover's embrace. Too inviting. Too aware.

I stretched, feeling muscle and bone snap awake, nerves vibrating with an unsettling vitality. My skin hummed with vibrant life and a sensitivity I had not felt before. The silk nightgown covering me felt like a violation, smooth and foreign against my freshly scrubbed skin.

Sliding aside the veil-like curtain, the oppressive room pressed in, cold and immaculate. A twisted Renaissance fantasy unfolded before me. A dark cathedral dedicated to forgotten gods hungering for blood. Three steps descended from the bed onto polished slate, partially hidden beneath an ornate rug woven in sinister shades of gold, black, green, and deep crimson.

Massive ebony furniture loomed, polished surfaces reflecting candle flames like distorted eyes watching my every move. Stone walls encased me completely, carved deep into the mountain's heart. No windows. No escape. Only oppressive gloom and flickering candlelight.

I snapped. I was exhausted from not feeling welcome in my own body. From the incessant voices constantly plaguing me. From the fight to survive in a strange new world where nothing was as it seems. Every moment I felt further away from myself and the strange presence in me grew louder.

"What the fuck is going on here?" I screamed, voice raw, echoing off stone walls, mocking my helplessness.

His laugh, cold, hollow, infused with rot and dark amusement. It crawled beneath my skin, nesting deep within my bones. The scent of death trailed him—ancient and knowing—as he filled the doorway with suffocating dominance. Damp black hair framed his face, absorbing the room's flickering light, killing its warmth. His amber gaze glowed with unsettling clarity—it sliced through me, laying my soul bare.

"My pet," he cooed. His tone a combination of amusement and patronizing. "No one will hear your cries. It pleases me to see you awake, somewhat coherent."

"I am not your pet. Stop treating me like a child!" I realized the ridiculousness of that statement when I stomped my foot on the mattress.

"Then stop acting like one." His smile was a corpse's grim parody of charm. "You will find clothes in the bureau. They should fit perfectly."

I snarled, hoping to stab him with my words. "How the hell do you know my size? Did you strip and measure me while I lay helpless?

Did you enjoy the show, you sick bastard? You still haven't told me who the fuck you are!"

The feelings of hate, rage, sorrow, grief, and…lust all surged through me. A muddied whirlwind of conflicting emotions pushed me closer to the edge. I crouched, coiling in on myself, like a lioness ready to pounce. Then he was there, impossibly fast, with an unnatural grace. His hands captured my wrists, mocking my vulnerability with that cruel half-smirk.

"Let's clarify something, pet," he purred dangerously. "I detest being threatened or attacked—especially in my own home. The clothes are here because I prefer my playthings… well adorned."

His voice sliced through my defiance, freezing me with dread, reminding me not so subtly of his absolute supremacy. He released me. His power radiating through his threat. I huffed and sat back on the bed.

"I. am. not. your. pet! I am not wearing someone's hand-me-downs just because you want me to play dress up." I couldn't hide the petulant tone in my voice and how childish it came across. Tears poked at my eyes as I fought the barrage of emotions I felt toward this man…this thing…my sire.

"While this defiant behavior is something you are used to doing… I am finding it rather irksome and it is pushing my patience. Get dressed," he ordered sharply. "We have guests. Choose something tasteful and try not to act like a feral beast."

He vanished without a sound, leaving me sprawled beneath the oppressive canopy, trembling with futile anger. I had to find a way out of this toxicity. Maybe I could stay long enough to learn how to control myself then I could break away. All I knew in this moment was I wanted…no *needed*…to get out. The feeling of foreboding sank heavily in my bones.

"Fuck you…" My whisper was brittle, cracked, by barely restrained fury. My fists slammed into the mattress, feet kicking wildly like a child's tantrum. "Who the fuck does he think he is?"

Rising unsteadily, the icy chill of the stone floor stung my bare feet, each step driving pins of pain upward, I approached the armoire. My fingers traced intricate carvings, cool, slick beneath my touch, silver filigree shimmered in the dim candlelight. Dragons frozen mid-roar stared back, their silent screams a cruel reminder of my own impotence.

Inside, lavender and cedar thickened the air—another seduction, another trap. Seven delicate dresses whispered alluring words of confidence as the fabric danced under the brush of my hand. My hand stopped at a long black gown shimmering with crystals and silver detailing—a dress fit for death's bride. Matching black strappy heels waited silently beneath.

The bathroom, stocked with lavish feminine trappings, felt sacred in a perverse way. I approached the mirror warily, dread pooling in my stomach. I had only seen myself a few times since I woke in this nightmare and each time, I struggled with recognition. Subtle, yet dramatic changes were all I saw each time I took the chance to gaze upon my reflection.

I froze.

The color of my hair had become more vibrant, almost glowing in an unnatural way. It looked silkier and softer than before, laying in waves over my shoulders. My skin no longer carried the blemishes of humanity, rather it had lightened, more alabaster than porcelain. Though that is not what threw me off…no it was the subtle black streaks along my veins, appearing and disappearing that caught my attention.

My eyes were another change I could not process. They too glowed with a vibrancy that was inhuman. However, the once black freckles in my irises had morphed into fissures. They appeared to move with a life of their own, creating shapes and patterns that distorted the colored rings. Even in the dim light, I could see clearly and where my pupils would have been dilated wide to allow for more light, they retained their baseline size. It felt like something sinister stared back at me from within those cracks, pressing against my mind, begging for release.

"What the fuck…" I paused as horror and awe mingled in a sour tone.

I reached for the makeup, deciding against foundation, rather settling on some mascara and eyeliner. The deep black tones contrasting against the violet. I stared at the various shades of lipstick, settling on a deep red. The dark color making my lips more pronounced, even sultry.

I don't know how long I sat there staring at my reflection. At this woman, I wanted to love even as much as I feared her. I knew if I sat here for too long, he would get angry and start calling for me, yet I could not move. I wanted to run. Needed to run. And for some reason, it was not going to be the choice I made. I was trapped in a cave turned domicile with a living, breathing myth.

What is wrong with me?

Chapter 11

Vakor

The moans and wet sighs drifting around the ballroom pierced my ears like hot wire—grating, indulgent, sloppy. Nails on slate would have been preferable. When we get to feed uninhibited and in privacy, some of us lose all decorum.

My "guests" had arrived barely an hour ago, and already they were tearing into the feeders like rabid dogs. No restraint. Only gluttony. I rolled my eyes at them.

Pathetic.

I exhaled—long, deliberate. "*Do try* to leave some of them intact until the whelp comes down," I said, voice dripping in disdain. "It would be a shame for her to miss the dining experience simply because you three drained them for sport."

The words fell from my lips like scalding oil, neither request nor reprimand. Just a reminder. I was the second eldest of the Canaanites and sometimes it felt like having to be the parent since our eldest sister was trapped somewhere in the human world.

"Vakor, darling," Iyzebel purred, her tone silk and daggers. "You really *must* loosen up. Why bother with such a splendid display if not to indulge our… baser appetites?"

Her voice was dipped in sin but held considerable weight. Had I not known her so well, her tone might've provoked a fight. She'd lost a tongue once for less. I smirked at the memory. The night Iyzebel lost her tongue for taunting War. He hated her and to this day threatened to behead her if he saw her again. She is one of the youngest of us and had many progenies scattered across the continents. She was also the most aloof.

"Indeed, Vakor," Abbadon rumbled, voice cold as the tundra. "You present such a feast… and yet forbid us to partake? These creatures exist for two things: *pleasure* and *sustenance*."

My eye twitched, slightly. Abbadon's presence always brought an ancient chill—blood-soaked and crawling up my spine like frostbite. He walked a strange line between light and dark thanks to his patronage. He was also the eldest of Lilith's children. I respected him as much as I feared him. In reality, we all had a healthy fear of each other. Our births and gifts as unique as we were, a small token from the shadows and Hell.

I rose from my chair. Stretching as I did. The weight of my immortality and new found whelp forcing muscles to tighten under the strain.

The wood groaned beneath me—solid ebony, carved by artisans who still bled for their craft. Every inch of this hall, five thousand square feet of gothic elegance, echoed my will. Queen Anne chairs formed a throne-like procession down the grand table. I always sat at the head. Naturally.

The ballroom and dining hall had hosted carnage masquerading as celebration for centuries. Tonight would be no different. When one of us sired a vampire, it was a big ordeal in the past. Now, it became almost second nature and recently, the drive to create was almost stronger than the desire to destroy. I was one of the few who did not like having to raise a whelp.

"Iyzebel," I said, voice clipped, "she'll descend soon. I *assume*." The word hissed like venom. "Modern women seem to think time bends to their whims. At least in past centuries, gowns required layers and servants. There was *justification* for their tardiness."

Where was the little bitch? I tried to stay calm and *gentle* with the girl, but there was a limit to my patience, and it was quickly nearing the end. I paced the dais, torn between waiting and dragging her defiant ass down the stairs dressed or not.

"Tuttle," I barked. The parasite shuffled forward like an insect. "The papers?"

"Yes, your lordship." That wheeze. That disgusting cough. He always sounded like he was trying—and failing—to die. "All prepared for her signature."

Tuttle had been rotting when I found him—drunk, diseased, collapsing in a piss-soaked opium den in Philadelphia. Once brilliant, he'd been top of his class, the first to graduate from that cesspool they called a law school in 1790. Yet, the unfettered debauchery of the times called to him more so than the oath he took.

I offered him a choice: die screaming or serve forever.

He, like most mortals, chose the predictable option. They all craved immortality. Their vanity and fear of death, and innate greed always pushing them to want more than what was within their limits. He still reeked of spoiled ambition. Five-foot-five of gluttony stuffed into a pinstriped suit. Sausage fingers, blotchy skin, hair greasy and perpetually frozen mid-decay.

And I *trusted him*—as far as a blade could penetrate his spine. He was a snake wrapped in deceptive packaging and most of our kind knew that of him. Hence the reason he was kept on a short leash.

"You transferred all of her liquid assets to Yakam's bank?" I asked. Watching as his eye twitched and his pallor grayed.

"All of it, yes, your lordship," he croaked. "I wouldn't dream of repeating past mistakes."

I smiled.

He remembered. The missing fingers on his left hand. The stump where his foot used to be. He had thought himself clever during the first internet boom—skimming fractions from my accounts and others like a rat nibbling cheese.

The foot was for fleeing. The fingers… for reaching where he shouldn't. While we can heal and regrow damaged or loss parts, withholding feeding stops the regrowth and slows the healing. He was provided with a prosthetic foot and a glove to cover his hand.

"See that you *continue* to not dream," I said coolly. "You may leave."

He paled. Good. I watched as he hobbled back over to the feeders, planting himself in front of a rather endowed young woman. His giggles of delight as he slapped and clawed her breasts caused me to feel queasy and wish for his death.

Some things even I do not enjoy watching…as I saw him pull his semi-erect penis from his trousers. The disgust sending chills down my spine.

Still no Kallea. Irritation clawed at my throat. My steps echoed like gunshots across the slate as I made my way to the staircase carved into the wall—a spiral of ancient stone, smooth from centuries of use.

This fortress had been mine for thousands of years. Buried within the Appalachian Mountains, cloaked in rock and shadow. I had chosen it when men still believed bears were gods. The cave called to me— hollowed, hidden, and patient. It has become a sanctuary and a place where we could meet without fear of discovery.

The world below could burn and we would be safe. Ancient magic warded it keeping humans and others at a safe distance. Venture too close and it would send soul crushing fear throughout the body, ultimately causing death. Only those with our blood could pass the barrier unscathed, unless directly invited. The irony of that was not lost on me considering the legends saying vampires could only enter if invited.

I steeled myself, leaning against the thick wooden banister. The distance up the stairs, covered in shadow, broken only by the twinkle of candlelight. I had my place wired for electricity when it was first discovered and updated as the technology grew…however, the harshness of the lighting did not appeal to my finer senses…so candlelight remained my only source of light. The whelp still had not appeared and what little resolve I had, faded.

Taking a deep breath and pushing all my power into the words, I commanded…

"*PET… NOW.*" My voice exploded upward. Rage seeped into my words, allowing them to *sting* as they climbed the walls.

I knew I should not be acting forcefully toward her, yet the unknown about her nagged at me. Too many things were not adding up and yet they were. If the signs were correct… we were in for one hell of a surprise.

Chapter 12

Kallea

"PET…NOW."

Vakor's voice slammed into me, rattling through the stone and slicing into my skull as if he stood right beside me. A low, dangerous growl vibrated deep in my throat, echoing my seething hatred for the monster who commanded me. And somehow resistance came easier this time.

"I AM NOT YOUR FUCKING PET!" I screamed, finally pissed off at his constant douchebag behavior. For fuck's sake that man was infuriating. How many times did I have to say that to him before he quit calling me it?

I made the decision, I would taunt that bastard and take my time. I rose from the vanity. Pausing to check my reflection one last time. The pristine elegance of my appearance belied the chaos raging inside me. Each step toward the door felt heavier than the last, trepidation coiled tight within my chest as Vakor's voice roared again.

"Pet, if you do not move those damned feet faster, I will personally drag your infantile ass down these FUCKING STEPS!" The final words erupted from every crack and crevice in the room reverberating like thunder, dislodging dust and debris that showered down, increasing my hesitation.

I paused at the door, my hand shaking as I reached for the handle. I knew he waited for me, but I was unsure about the guests he said were going to be here. I didn't even know where here was and that scared me more than the idea of being met by more monsters. He called himself a Canaanite. A being separate from vampires but the same. Were these guests the same as him or were they creatures from other…species? With a final deep breath, I opened the door.

The instant my foot touched the first step, the faint strains of music crept toward me—*Mozart's Requiem*—an elegant melody twisted to the grotesque by the sinister atmosphere. I descended, my hand brushing the cool, unyielding stone wall, its chill seeping into my fingertips, whispering promises of long time captivity.

Candle flames flickered within small alcoves, their dancing light casting ominous, shifting shadows concealing threats lurking just out of sight. The swirls of color from the stone created a psychedelic dance in the flickering lights. Each tap of my heels echoed harshly, discordant against the smooth, melodic symphony, amplifying the growing pressure in my chest.

The stairs ended in a vast foyer carved crudely yet majestically from the mountain's black heart. It was the only place I could fathom we would be due to the stone surrounding us. But where these mountains were, I did not know. I gritted my teeth as I continued to take in the site, tamping down the storm of emotions threatening to overpower me.

Towering ceilings rose high, swallowing candlelight greedily. An opulent runner stretched from enormous ebony double doors to an imposing arched entryway, its rich black interwoven with sickly shades of red, gold, and green. I stood frozen, entranced by the twisted grandeur until Vakor's chilling voice violently dragged me back to reality.

"Ah, my pet. So glad you decided to join us. That dress suits you impeccably. You look positively ravishing."

He emerged from the shadows, radiating predatory elegance, dark hair pulled tautly back, his tailored suit clinging obscenely to his muscular form, the open collar hinting at the lethal strength beneath. His eyes cut through me, stirring a perverse mix of terror and lust.

"Where the hell am I?" I snarled. "And why am I here? Answer me, damn you!"

His mere presence rattled me. His scent thick with old death, blood, and malicious intent. My nails bit painfully into my palms, gums aching as emotion and hunger surged through me. Red blurred my vision. Images of violence mingled with dark, forbidden desires in a deadly dance. My mind torn between ripping out his throat and falling helplessly into his ruthless embrace.

"Mmm… Vakor, who is this exquisite creature?"

The disembodied voice purred in my ears from somewhere in the adjoining room. Its melodic tone weaved in time with the chords of music, deepening its allure. Raising my alarm further. I turned, and watched as the most picturesque woman stepped from the shadows. Her posture and walk radiated ethereal elegance with a murderous undertone. She was old. Very old…

Her ivory skin glowed beneath cascading white curls. Her voluptuous curves confined within an emerald gown. The corseted top barely containing her lush form. Crimson nails, sharp as talons, gleamed as the dim light caught them. Diamond jewelry glittering upon her fingers.

"Lower your hackles, ma petite," she said with gentle indifference, extending her hand. Her voice carried a faint, ancient, possibly French, accent, edged with a hidden threat. "I won't bite… yet. It appears Vakor is a neglectful host. I am Iyzebel."

"Kallea," I replied. Silently slapping myself for how meek and timid I sounded. Just call me Courage the Cowardly Vampire. Regret was instantaneous as her grip tightened to the point of pain. My bones nearly shattering beneath her delicate fingers.

I yanked my hand back, stepping away as a torrent of emotions washed through me. Standing before two lethal predators, I was acutely aware of my vulnerability. And despite my revulsion, I found myself drawn toward the darkness radiating from them. Craving the very thing that threatened to consume me, mind and body.

The gleam in their eyes betrayed that they could scent my heightened arousal, just as surely as I felt the moisture gathering in expectation between my thighs. How could two so frighteningly dangerous monsters be so damn intoxicating? I wanted to be them as much as I wanted to just be me again. Although, who I was had now become a past memory.

I would be forgotten by time, mourned by few, and ignored by the rest. This was my life now and I had no choice but to embrace it. But how? How would I be able to turn off the piece of me that still craved life? Craved human connection…the sun…the embrace of love…everything I would be denied in this new life.

Vakor would not love me. He barely tolerated me. I was expendable if I did not conform. Realizing my human life with Anthony had been a lie just cemented the reality that I was unloved and unwanted by anyone who was not my parents. I was nothing then and I am nothing now. It was a jagged pill to swallow, yet it was the bitter truth.

"She smells familiar. Vakor, where did you find her?" Vakor leveled an icy glare in Izyebel's direction. A silent demand to shut up, one that she appeared to not read, or she just simply ignored it. "I do say, ma petite, there is an oldness to your scent. One that is tickling my memory."

"Izyebel." That one word. Her name spoken in a stab laced warning. Not deep enough to be fatal, but enough to catch her attention.

I looked at him wide eyed. Confusion screaming at me and an all too familiar pulsing in the back of my mind. *Oldness? What does she mean by that? How can I be familiar when we have never met? Can she smell my insanity?* My thoughts were interrupted by a strange noise coming from Izyebel's lips.

Her laugh came out broken by discomfort as she worked to regain her composure. It was becoming more and more obvious that Vakor held authority and even one who was his equal would back down. I looked between the two of them not knowing what to say or do, or if I should do anything. The tension radiated off of them worse than enemies forced into a truce.

I knew in that moment, I either submitted and thrived or die. His imposing nature promised that with no further words needed. And how I wanted to give him all the words…

Chapter 13

Unknown

I am the First. The Beginning. The inevitable End.

From my shadow, nightmares were borne; from my darkness, all light shall be extinguished. The night air hung heavy with the intoxicating aroma of life—vibrant, desperate, and blind to impending doom. Humans passed through their fleeting existence, oblivious cattle awaiting slaughter. Fine wine, *they* named it; to me, merely sustenance.

A dark chuckle escaped me, a low rumble reverberating softly as I melted into the alley's gloom, irresistibly drawn by the scent of recent death and mortal sin. Yellow human barriers fluttered uselessly—pathetic attempts to shroud mortal frailty. With contemptuous ease, I tore the door from its hinges, metal shrieking in futile protest.

The pungent stench of violence struck me instantly—blood, decay, and reckless abandon. Under it all, the scent of age, immortality, and youth lingered. Unrestrained fury surged through me. Foolish spawn, leaving their prey half-devoured and exposed. Walls, ceiling, and floor bore a grotesque testimony to their carelessness.

A sharp hiss escaped me as I silently vowed to teach these impudent fledglings the true meaning of fear and consequence. Carelessness like this was an untenable violation of our secrecy.

Suddenly, muted voices intruded upon my senses, accompanied by faint, uncertain footsteps that echoed against concrete and brick. Two officers, mortal pawns feigning bravery, entered. The wavering beams of their lights betrayed unease, illuminating hesitant movements and cowering souls.

"Police—show yourself!" The male strained, authority slipping away as tremors revealed his unease.

I remained unseen, savoring their mounting dread as the scent of anxiety bloomed in the air. The female spoke, her voice tight with barely restrained panic. "Jugs, something feels wrong. Can we leave? Please?"

"Yeah, Mish." Jugs replied. His increasing anxiety pushing his eyes to dart frantically through oppressive shadows. "It feels… like the darkness is swallowing the light."

Another low chuckle emerged from me. The sound bouncing from every shadowed crevice. Both mortals froze, the audible sound of their hammering hearts gaining volume. Their dread kicking their fight or flight instincts into a higher gear. Light beams quivered as desperate fingers clenched. I could feel their minds unraveling in terror.

They began to retreat, each hurried step surrendering further to their primitive need to survive. I drifted without sound behind them. The shadows swelling at my silent command. A living darkness devouring their feeble illumination. Jugs sensed it first, his voice extinguished abruptly as eternal night engulfed him.

His mouth opened, a scream dying before it reached his lips, by my iron grip upon his throat. His eyes widened, limbs thrashed helplessly as I drained the vitality from him. His desiccated body fell to the ground, a hollow, soulless thud reverberating through the corridor.

"Jugs?" Mish's voice cracked, hysteria shredding her composure. Her beam swung in frantic arcs, searching for her vanished companion. Sweat glistened on her trembling dark skin, breath heaving beneath cumbersome attire. "Jugs! Answer me!"

The exquisite aroma of her terror filled my senses—intoxicating, ripe, begging to be consumed. She turned to flee, and I surged forward, shadows ensnaring her, silencing her futile resistance. She fought weakly, gasping, sobbing, until I drained her as thoroughly as the last.

Striking a match against the rough brick, I tossed it into the dark hallway and beckoned the shadows. They responded, eager for destruction, gathering the flames and spreading them throughout the building. In mere moments, all evidence of the spawn's recklessness was obliterated, hidden beneath the cleansing inferno.

The moon hung full and treacherous. The sky accursedly clear. The fall air a cool breath against my perpetually hot skin. How unfortunate. I clung to the bricks, allowing mortal constructs to shield me from heaven's prying gaze. The scent of the spawn tugged insistently at me—stronger now, closer.

I quickened my pace, cloaked by darkness, eternal ally of my kind.

I am shadow. I am rot. I am the terror gods themselves feared enough to bury.

And now, I rise again.

The world has forgotten its predator.

It shall soon remember.

These spawn—these "vampires"—have desecrated our legacy. They breed without reverence. They exist without purpose.

Their existence ends now.

Chapter 14

Kallea

I felt like I was suffocating. Breath would not come, and the room began to spin. I ran to the towering entry doors, throwing them open and practically falling through to the outside. I needed air. I needed to run, even knowing I would not get far. I collapsed to the ground, the cold, thin air choking me as I gulped it like it was the only way to live. The tears I had fought to contain burst free, soaking the ground.

I heard their steps as loudly as I felt their presence behind me. I don't know how, but I could feel Vakor's disgust and disappointment in me, and it made me cry harder. I could not stop the oppressive feeling that was consuming me. I wanted to go home, and I knew this was now my home—at least until he tired of me and killed me.

"I have no intention of killing you, pet. Not yet, at least." The truth in his words offered little comfort. I knew the pregnant pause came with a but. "I may dislike this display of humanity and as long as you keep it to a minimum, you will live."

And there it was, the demand. Shed the last of my humanity. The last thread keeping me tethered to the life I lost. "How?" I hiccupped through ragged sobs.

"Let us show you, ma petite. I, for one, would love to introduce you to all the decadence immortality can bring. Especially the sensual parts." Her lust-laden purr ignited heat between my thighs and a strange tingling in my stomach.

Standing, my back still to them, I stared off into the abyss of the mountain range. It was then I realized just how scarce the air was this high up and how little it affected me. Had I still been human, it would not take long, weeks maybe, for me to go cyanotic and eventually die from lack of oxygen. Even the frigid temperature did not bother me.

When I turned, Vakor's mouth tightened into something I did not want to name, malicious amusement glittering in his amber eyes. "My dear Iyzebel, we are missing the festivities—and I know how you loathe being left out." His gaze flicked briefly to mine, a silent challenge. "Come along, pet. We have guests eager for your introduction."

"No," I snarled, forcing my shaky legs to hold steady. "I'm done with the games. Tell me what's going on. No more dodging."

A deadly quiet settled between us. Vakor's eyes hardened, flashing with promises of violence. "Pet," he hissed, stepping so near his breath brought goosebumps to my skin, "have you forgotten what I can, and will, do to you should you defy me again? Now move."

My resolve wavered under the crushing weight of his threat, yet I clenched my jaw, clinging to…I don't know what… "No."

"Fine," he sighed, exasperation etched across his face as he tilted toward the sky, scraping one hand down it. His patience had reached its limit. Without another word, he seized my arm and pulled me unwillingly through the foyer into the large room beyond.

The moment we crossed the threshold, the music, Beethoven, struck my ears, a bright, saccharine melody juxtaposed with the unfolding nightmare. The cavernous room exuded opulence—high vaulted ceilings, extravagant round tables, flickering candlelight. But decadence twisted abruptly into depravity.

I froze.

Eight mortals stood arranged beneath the chandeliers like offerings laid upon an altar. Their limbs were restrained with deliberate artistry—wrists stretched, throats collared, ankles secure. Not chaos. Design.

Their cries rose beneath the swell of Beethoven—distorted, gagged, swallowed by refinement. The music did not clash with their suffering. It elevated it.

A woman shrieked as a man stepped onto the bench, the crude rasp of his zipper jarring obscenely against the refined backdrop. Horror surged inside me, choking my breath, yet beneath it rose a sickening, uninvited sensuality.

Every instinct screamed at me to turn away. To claw my own eyes blind. To puncture my ears, welcoming the deafening silence.

Instead, I stepped closer.

My pulse did not race from fear alone. Something inside me leaned forward, curious. Hungry. The sound of flesh meeting flesh echoed like a heartbeat I could not silence.

"Does it repulse you," Vakor murmured against my ear, "or does it call to you?"

His voice slid into the spaces my conscience could no longer defend.

"No, not disgusted," he continued softly. "You are becoming."

"Mmmm, *ma petite*, you must join in. Vakor has yet to disappoint with his selection." Iyzebel's chest rose and fell with passion, eyes hooded as she devoured the scene before us, lost to the surrounding debauchery.

"Frederick has always been an ass man. He prefers the tight restraint versus the soft supplication of a woman's cunt."

I moaned, breath catching as I melted into Vakor. My back met his chest—unyielding, immovable. This was no tender moment. It was a wicked waltz of desire and will, where softness meant surrender, and I was falling fast. Every last drop of fight attempting to flee under the salacity of the scene before me.

Closing my eyes, I let the mood settle over me. I wanted to give in…to let this predator in me free…but my lingering humanity waged war, refusing to cede to our darker side. And yet, I caved.

Vakor's hands moved languidly over my body. The faintest of brushes grazed the swell of my breasts, unbound beneath silk, before gliding lower, each stroke drawing a whispered friction between fabric and skin.

His breath caressed me like a lover's promise—one I craved and feared all at once. Iyzebel traced her fingers down my cheek. The delicate touch was a cruel contrast to the lethality of her nails. Her lips brushed softly against mine. My own parted in a sigh as her tongue drew across them, seeking permission. I welcomed the kiss—devouring it. I wanted to drown in it, to lose myself, to forget everything but this wicked dance with two of the most dangerous creatures in history.

The feeling of her tongue rolling over mine sent warm pulses to my core, drawing another lust-filled moan from me. She tasted of crimson, of life and death, purity and evil. My desire increased into a raging fire, as her fingers found my nipples, pinching and pulling them.

The wanton arch of my body pushed my breasts deeper into her grasp. Our hips met…rubbing against each other. Seeking the release I knew was just on the edge of my awareness. *Oh gawd. This, this is perfection and I want more.*

Vakor's hands slid down my sides, slow and taunting, bunching up the length of my dress, exposing me to the room. He held the gathered fabric with one hand while his other hand trailed an agonizing path to my core. His fingers traced delicate patterns around my sensitive, aching nub. The deliberate avoidance of direct contact drove me to maddening heights.

A chill greeted me as one of Iyzebel's hands left my breast and followed the same path as Vakor. Her fingers joined his, and my mind shattered from the sensory onslaught. I cried out as one of her fingers plunged so deep in me, her knuckles pressed my core. Adding another finger had my knees faltering as shock waves rippled from the soles of my feet, colliding with the building ache in my abdomen.

My head hit Vakor's chest as I threw it back in an orgasmic scream. My muddied mind barely made out his chuckle in my ear. A soft breeze fluttered around me as Iyzebel moved away. The skirt of my dress fell back around my legs. Every brush sending goosebumps and sparks throughout my sensitive body.

Vakor's fingers gripped my chin, lifting my drooping head to face the captive humans in front of us. "Watch her…see how she commands ecstasy and control. You can be her, if only you surrender."

The truth of his words sank in and as much as I wanted to let go, I knew I couldn't give in completely. I wasn't a monster…at least…that is what I thought. My satiated mind wanted to watch, to lose myself in this sick and twisted perversion while a small part of me wanted to run away.

Iyzebel approached a dark-skinned male who trembled helplessly against his restraints, erection pulsing in forced arousal. With terrifying grace, she tore away her clothing, standing bare and magnificent. Her porcelain skin gleamed like cold marble.

Her lips parted, fangs glinting in the candle glow, as she leaned forward and sank her mouth onto his cock. Blood trickled down his shaft, mingling with her saliva as she bobbed her head up and down, drinking from him, until he cried out in release. I watched, trapped by the sight of her throat's movement as she swallowed his release.

My stomach churned with revulsion, even as my mind began to cave to the perverse fascination gripping my senses. The aroma of sex, sweat, and blood saturated the air like thick poison, intoxicating yet vile.

I found myself moving, as if pulled by an outside force, closer to the human display. The young blond man strapped tightly to a table stared at me. Terror glistened in his wide, desperate eyes. He smelled earthy and sweet—sandalwood, honeysuckle, fear. My mouth watered as I brushed a fingernail along his straining erection, my own arousal no longer denied. Leaning in, I inhaled deeply, my fangs aching, desire and hunger waging a savage war within, tearing away the last bit of my resolve.

"Do you desire him?" Vakor's excited whisper coiled into my ear.

"No… *Yes*." My voice was thick and heavy.

"Then take him." The gravel in his voice chipped away at the barrier of my self-control.

Cold fingers caressed my skin, tracing the delicate straps of my gown until they slipped down my arms, the dress pooling silently at my feet. Naked and exposed, my nipples tightened painfully, every inch of me vibrating under Vakor's possessive touch. Before I could gather my senses, Vakor's hands seized my waist, lifting me effortlessly, only to slam me down onto the bound man's cock. A cry tore from my lips at the sudden heat invading me as rapture collided with pain.

His voice, wicked with amusement yet thick with longing, whispered against my ear, "Have you ever wondered what it feels like to ride a man as he is defiled?"

My insides twisted with a blend of horror and excitement as Vakor moved behind me, violating the young man's innocence. His screams of pain reverberated through my bones before collapsing into unwilling moans. The rhythm of my movements controlled by Vakor's brutal thrusts, each a savage punctuation of depravity.

Another vampire approached silently, his white hair cascading over his shoulders in sultry waves, hiding his monstrous nature. Pale fingers traced down the young man's chest before settling against the raw ache between my thighs. His ministrations deepened the cruel torment of my body…my mind.

Throwing my head back, I released a cry as it tore from my chest, my mind consumed by the carnal sensations pulsing through me. As I screamed through my release, I knew, in that moment, I would give in to him, to the malevolence inside me, to anything just to keep this pleasure for eternity.

Warmth flooded my mouth—I had bitten into his flesh without realizing, my face pressed into the crook of the feeder's neck. The taste intoxicated me, heady and hot, sharp with life. I hummed in pleasure at the multitude of sensations as each of Vakor's thrusts pushed the young man's hips up into me. The movement forced rushes of blood down my throat. I was so lost in all of it that even the lurking presence stirring within did not faze me.

"Feed," Vakor urged. He lifted me, holding tight to him as I found my balance. His hand pressed between my shoulder blades, guiding my face downward—not gently, not cruelly, but inevitably. My fangs descended, mouth sealing around the man's length.

The first taste was not human. It was something darker. Myself reflected back through him. I recoiled. Then swallowed. Pressure built within me and as Vakor took me from behind, I erupted. His movements, possessive and cruel, held me frozen in place.

The climax was not release. It was fracture. Something inside me, fragile, human, pleading, snapped like a bone under pressure. And when it did, the shadows surged in triumph. I did not fight them. I let them take the space that was left.

Chapter 15

Vakor

The way she yielded to pain and pleasure was a perfection that captivated me. Her body flushed from the echoes of every climax. I had coaxed each one from her. Her breath came in soft, ragged whimpers as I held her against my chest, her legs unsteady from exhaustion. A smile crept across my face. I knew the moment she had finally surrendered to this life. The way she had leaned into the feeder, biting him as I had taught her, stirred a dark pride in me.

With reluctant gentleness, I carried her to the dais and settled her carefully on my lap at the head of the table. Flushed and glistening with sweat and arousal, she trembled slightly in my arms. I retrieved a warm towel from the heated tray beside me, running it over her sensitive skin, marveling at the stark contrast between her soft flesh and my cold hands.

These decadent gatherings were not new to me: the feeders arrived eagerly, enticed by money and hollow promises, wholly unaware they'd remember nothing of their degradation. Vampire venom was superior in its efficiency: a potent trifecta of ecstasy, submission, and amnesia—ensuring effortless control.

"You still owe me answers, Vakor," Kallea murmured, a weariness lacing her words. Her violet eyes, half-lidded yet fiercely vibrant, shimmered with the aftershocks of her climaxes. But as I looked closer, I noticed a disquieting shift. Within those violet pools, tendrils of black twisted and danced, morphing them, granting them a life of their own. My senses sharpened, alert, and wary. Something was changing inside her. I felt the cold dread of a still-hidden familiarity crawling up my spine. Only one of us had blood of black and shadow… and though my pet was not her… this unsettled me.

"You're right, pet," I conceded, pushing aside the unease stirring deep within my chest. "I'll grant you answers. Ask carefully, one at a time."

"Why me?" Her voice, barely a whisper, tremulous with lingering fear and vulnerability. But beneath it simmered defiance and anger. Traits I secretly hoped she retained. The way she curled into me showed her submission to our bond and to me as her sire.

I chuckled darkly. "Opportunity, my pet. Your car crashed on that isolated mountain road I frequently traveled." The memory flashed with clarity in my mind. "I caught the acrid scent of smoke and heard your broken cries as your life slipped away. I intended merely to feed, grant you a swift death, and move on."

Pausing, I savored the confusion and horror flickering across her delicate features. "Yet, as I was about to depart, you grabbed my arm—your dying grip stronger than it had any right to be. You pleaded weakly for me to stay."

Her eyes widened with curiosity, her body shifting instinctively closer until she straddled me oblivious to how my cock strained, trapped between our heated bodies. Her breasts, supple and youthful, sculpted perfectly to fit my hand. The deep brown of her nipples stood out stark against porcelain skin. Unblemished. Tempting. Mine.

"Then, some fool human struck me with a branch, no more than an irritation, yet enough to split my lip and spill my blood," I sneered, vividly recalling the humiliating blow. "And thus, your fate was sealed. You do not become a vampire from a mere bite—you must hover at the brink of death. Your soul poised on the precipice of leaving your body. Only then can our blood permit the shades to force the frail human essence from your mortal shell."

At the mention of the word 'shade,' she went rigid, muscles tensing enticingly against me. She writhed in panic, whimpers and soft cries escaping, stimulating the predator deep within me. The aroma of her fear and anger permeated the room, and the vampires around me inhaled sharply, nostrils flaring, eyes darkening, lips curled back baring fangs.

"Calm yourself, pet," I warned sharply, tightening my grip possessively. "Your anger is arousing to our kind—we feast on strong emotions. Do not provoke the frenzy."

She swallowed hard, fear and caution chasing away the anger, until it simmered just beneath the surface. Still, she persisted, unrelenting in her pursuit for the truth. "So, you made me a demon who feeds on blood and must fuck to feel anything? Why not kill me that night in that filthy bar? Why spare me?"

I laughed softly, admiring the intoxicating blend of innocence and corruption warring within her. "You misunderstand, my little pet. The demon, as you call it, is simply a catalyst—it purges the human soul. Once expelled, it departs. The remnants of angelic essence in human flesh repel true possession. Vampire venom and shade work in harmony briefly. Nothing more." The look on her face remained defiant and expectant. "To answer your other question. Something about you intrigued me and it has been countless centuries since I last sired a vampire."

Her skeptical eyes locked on mine. A sarcastic smile curled at her lips. "Yet, if my soul is gone…why do I still feel human?"

"The soul leaves, but its residue lingers for decades," I explained patiently, possessively caressing the smooth curve of her waist. "It takes nearly a century for the last sparks of humanity to fade completely. Human souls are woven with trace amounts of angelic essence—it permeates their blood, muscles, and bones. When we feed it fights with our venom, creating a powerful aphrodisiac. This is why humans crave our bite after the first."

"How old are you exactly?" she asked, the giggle in the question piercing the tension. Iyzebel's musical laughter echoed beside us, drawing both our attention. The temptress climbed onto the table and sat, spreading her legs to frame Kallea. Her fingers danced over Kallea's shoulders, unmistakably sexual. My pet stiffened beneath her touch before leaning back into it.

"We predate modern humanity, ma petite," Iyzebel purred into her ear. Her hands lingered on the tender curve of her breasts, eliciting a quiet gasp from Kallea. "Older than nations, younger than Eden. We are Canaanites—the original vampires."

Confusion misted across Kallea's gaze, her struggle to remain focused wavering as Iyzebel's touch grew more provocative. Seizing the opportunity, I drew my tongue languidly over Kallea's nipple, eliciting a throaty moan that had my cock aching beneath her. With calculated grace, I positioned her, thrusting upward, driving into her as she gasped and shuddered atop me.

"Canaanites?" she echoed breathlessly. Her eyes flashed with turmoil, then softened under the weight of her arousal. "Vakor has said this before."

"Yes," I growled against her heated skin, rolling my hips to savor her exquisite tightness. "Descendants of Cain and Lilith. The first true vampires."

She shivered, her body arching into me, as I deepened my strokes, my grip bruising her hips in dominance. Her breath quickened, words dissolving as I rocked her mercilessly against me. I reveled in her surrender, watching the shadows deepen in those mesmerizing eyes. Lines of black flitted across her face, following the path of her veins— so brief, it was almost unnoticeable. I had to bite back a gasp of shock as I returned to the pleasure of the moment.

My voice sank, rough and low, the predator in me fully unleashed. "You will learn, my pet. You will embrace what you have become. There is no escape, only endless hunger and eternal pleasure."

She whimpered softly, her head thrown back in surrender, mine completely. I growled as I thrust into her, claiming her further, and binding her irrevocably to my darkness.

A cruel smile tugged at my lips as her cries filled the chamber, watching her yield completely, submitting to the monstrous truth of what she now was—my creation, my pet, mine.

My eyes followed Iyzebel's fingers as they dragged across Kallea's body, twisting and pulling her nipples. She sucked on her neck, an intimate kiss with no bite. Her fingers moved to circle and tend to her clit while I maintained my relentless rhythm. Kallea's muscles tensed, her inner walls fluttering as another orgasm built.

I pulled her from Iyzebel's grasp and licked the hollow where her neck met her shoulder. Feeling her tongue mimic mine drew a quiet chuckle from me, and then I sank my fangs in. Her orgasm-fueled screams dragged me over the edge with her. They ceased abruptly as she mirrored my action, biting into me. The intensity of the orgasm that tore through me came out in a muffled roar as I continued to suckle on my bite.

"My turn…" Abbadon's voice pulled me from my bliss, filling me with rage. He lifted Kallea with ease, not waiting for her to cling to him before he drove into her.

He nuzzled the curve of her neck, inhaling deeply before sinking his fangs into her. His eyes, closed in pleasure, snapped open in alarm. He pulled back, turning his gaze to me, silently communicating a discussion that was about to happen.

As he roared his release, he pushed Kallea back to prevent her from biting him, a whimper falling from her blood-stained lips. He kissed her while he moved her from him, laying her on the table, allowing Iyzebel a turn with our little pet.

"You…" Abbadon growled, pointing at me—rage rolled off him in waves as he stalked toward me. "What. is. she?"

"I have no idea what you mean, Abbadon. She is a whelp." My voice hitched, betraying my attempt at nonchalance. I knew there was something in her blood, though its origin eluded me.

"Do not lie to me, brother. What is her gift?" The tone of his voice left no room for deception.

"She can hear the shades. I doubt she even realizes those are the whispers she hears, though she can shut them out when her hunger is sated."

Abbadon's eyes widened. "Dora…"

Chapter 16

Kallea

I couldn't move. The feel of Iyzebel's fingers pushed inside me arched my back off the cold table. Her lips dancing over the hardened peaks of my breasts, trailing down to the apex of my thighs. Hushed and angry whispers teased at my ears, drowned out by the pounding of my heart and the rushing of blood through my veins.

"Mmm. Ma petit, you are delectable. I know now why Vakor has taken such a liking to you. You smell like a distant memory." The piercing of fangs at my inner thigh pulled a cry from me. Electric shocks ripped through me as I orgasmed…again and again. "You taste…"

The words paused on her lips and I felt the cool chill of the air kissing the space she left. My head fought me as I lifted the weighted boulder to find Iyzebel staring at me. Shock…and something else…distorted her face. Was it apprehension? Fear? Pushing myself up to where I sat in front of her, I traced my fingers along her hips…my mouth salivating at the thought of tasting her flesh.

What is wrong with me?

Why am I thinking about this?

The frenzy that had consumed the chamber only moments before seemed to recede, but not completely. The music still played, yet it felt distant now—warped, as though filtered through stone and marrow. The air was thick with the scent of sex and blood, but beneath it lingered something older. Metallic. Stagnant. Watching.

The shadows along the edges of the room no longer writhed in playful indulgence. They had stilled.

And I realized—they were not reacting to us.

They were listening.

A hiss left her mouth as I latched onto her nipple…sucking…and swirling my tongue around the velvet nub. My fangs scratched, drawing forth the rich claret from her skin. Fingers drawing to her center, I pushed into her wet nether region, curling and stroking the sensitive spot hidden inside. Her moans grew and turned to shouts of pleasure as I bit down, drawing her essence into me.

Delectation…sweet waves crashed down around both of us. Extra hands, touching, fondling me, fingers delving deep within me. Another puncture on my shoulder. Sounds of depraved gratification swirling around me…coming from me.

"Iyzebel. I am hurt at you keeping her to yourself, now that Vakor has decided to share. Should you not extend the same courtesy." The husky voice caressed me. I sighed, leaning back into the hard chest as we continued to give and receive. "Her blood has such an exquisite pungency of aged wine."

"Iyzebel." That one word. Her name spoken in a stab laced with warning. Not deep enough to be fatal but enough to catch her attention.

Frederick's tone carried its usual arrogance, but there was something beneath it. A subtle restraint. His gaze flicked not to me, but past me. Toward the far corner of the chamber where the candlelight struggled to reach.

His nostrils flared slightly. He smelled something. And he did not like it.

"Frederick, my love. We do not always need to share. I am growing rather fond of this pet." Her voice laced with amusement, as her eyes danced over me. "Besides, don't you have something to attend to? A certain fauteur de troubles of the loups variety…"

"N'en parlons pas. Anubis est pour le moins problématique."

I froze as their strange words swirled around me. I knew she sounded French and could understand she was something about trouble and…wolf(?)… and he clearly said the name Anubis and problem. Tension met my back as he stiffened behind me. Then, emptiness.

I watched the globes of his ass as it swayed with each step he took. His peach toned skin glowed in the flickering candlelight, dark chocolate brown hair pointing widely from his head, muscles rippling as he moved. Sex and death on two legs.

Iyzebel ran a warm cloth over me, cleaning away the drying rivulets of blood and semen. Her touch was gentler now. Not affectionate. Calculated. Her eyes studied me in a way they had not before.

"You have questions child."

It was not a question; it was a directed statement. I had so many questions begging to be asked, yet I could not form a single coherent thought. Everything felt surreal and foggy. My gaze lingered on her face, eyes squinted in thought as she continued her attentions.

"What is wrong with my blood?" It was a foolish question, yet it was one that pricked me. Vakor and her both said my blood tasted strange… "and what did you and Frederick say?"

"You are an inquisitive creature, are you not? First, nothing is wrong with your blood, it is different than most mortals. As we would say it is kissed by something otherworldly." A worry line formed between her brows as she drew them together. Pinched with thought. "Second, what we said was not for your ears."

The sharpness of that last statement halted any further push from me. Though, more questions arose from her statement of my *'being kissed'.*

"What do you mean 'kissed by something otherworldly'?"

She hesitated for half a breath too long. That was new. Iyzebel did not hesitate.

"It means that at some point in your ancestry, a human mated with something inhuman."

Confusion rolled in my mind, and I could not help the blank stare. Something inhuman…could vampires or Canaanites procreate with humans?

"Oh, silly child… not one of us. We cannot impregnate, nor become pregnant by a human. That is left to the others."

"How…"

Her laughter filled the room, eyes squinted, and all teeth on display. She glowed with amusement, and yet…there was death in her eyes.

"Did I know your next question? Well, it was the obvious direction…No? There are…how do you say…werewolves, witches, angels, and those of their ilk that can mate with humans. We, however, are, as your myths put it, dead, so no life will come from us…except through a blood exchange."

She sat in the chair vacated by Vakor, twirling her fingers over my knee. As she spoke, the temperature shifted, subtle but undeniable. The shadows along the ceiling seemed to contract. Not retreat. Condense.

"Werewolves are real? Witches? Angels?"

As if I should be shocked considering I was a fucking vampire. Yet the thought that all of this was real and existed among mortals was like having a bucket of ice water dumped on your head. It was brain overload, leaving more questions in its wake.

"Yes, werewolves are actually Hellhounds. They are Lucifer's personal guardians and the primary guards of Hell's gates. Witches are descendants of the protectors…well the ones who strayed from His divine path. And we all know where those vile do gooders come from…" Her tone shifted at the word protectors. Hatred laced it, not the theatrical kind, no this was old hatred. A festering rot that invaded a person's core.

Huh, guess they really are enemies. I still could not get my head to wrap around it. It felt like I was being pulled into another world…a nightmare of epic proportions—stealing me away from reality. Though this was my reality, and who the hell was she to tell me that what they were talking about was not for my ears.

What the fuck, I was going to ask anyway…

"Who is Anubis? I thought he was the Egyptian god who guarded tombs and guided souls to the Underworld. Will I ever meet him?" I knew my mythology as it was always something that fascinated me, and to know there were elements of truth to it, excited me.

"Excusez-moi? No…no…no. You do not want to meet him. He is Lucifer's headguard. The deadliest of his kind and sire to all Lycans." It was not difficult to notice the sneer lacing her words. It only added to the perplexity of the conversation. "Many myths and legends are based off reality, twisted to allow for the feeble minds of mortals to grasp the concepts. Anubis is no different. Though he did enjoy spending his time with many queens back in those days."

I did not miss the soft undertone of remembrance in her words. More questions lingered at the forefront of my mind, ready to break through the gate of my mouth. Yet, no words would come forth as a dark frostiness burrowed into my awareness---and from how still Iyzebel went—she felt it too. Her hand froze where it rested on my thigh. Her pupils dilated, though not with lust. With recognition.

Something dangerous was here…

The music did not stop. The mortals still moaned. But beneath it all, something older than the chamber itself had shifted.

And for the first time since I met her, I saw fear touch Iyzebel's face.

Chapter 17

Unknown

Copper. Blood. Death.

The scent was intoxicating—an alluring dance of violence and decay that filled my senses, tugging me toward its source. Sharp rock met the soft, velvet of snow in contradiction, painting a false depiction of the horrors it hid. The brightness of the full moon created a kaleidoscope of dark and light throughout the jagged surface. Shadows slithered amongst the crevices, beckoning me, whispering of those who hide behind the veil of stone.

The mountain did not sleep. It waited. The wind that curled around its peaks carried more than cold—it carried memory. And memory carried blood.

My steps left steaming footprints in the white carpeting as I approached my destination. Before me stood a stone fortress embedded into the sheer face of a mountain. Cold and unyielding, it provided a stronghold built to conceal the darkness it housed. The massive wooden doors, carved with intricate dragons frozen mid-roar, stood as a foreboding warning to intruders. Humans would have trembled, cowered, or fled from the power pulsing off the slabs. But I felt only contempt, a sinister amusement at their pathetic attempts to ward off nightmares.

The fortress was no mere shelter. It was a monument. A sanctuary forged for protection from God's burning wrath. The sun—His futile, vengeful attempt at punishing Lucifer and those who thrived in shadows. And yet, how beautifully it backfired. We did not merely survive in darkness; we flourished, we conquered, we dominated. Our defiance mocked His will. Our continued existence the bane of His, a reminder of His failure. He created light and called it good. He was the catalyst to our creation and called us mistake. How small His language has always been.

My hand touched the heavy doors. The scent of indulgence leaked from beneath the threshold. Decadence. Foolishness. Discipline abandoned. They opened without a sound, yielding to the primordial force flowing through my veins. I stepped into the vast, dimly lit chamber, my footsteps silent, absorbed by the stone floor that seemed to bow in reverence beneath me. The air was thick, saturated with the rich aroma of sex, sweat, blood, and fear. It embraced me, welcomed me, as I drew nearer to the dark archway ahead. Shadows laid a path before me, guiding me to my kin on the other side. My return was still unknown to them, and unwelcome.

Inside, dim candlelight flickered mockingly against the ancient stone, failing to fully banish the shadows that clung to corners and crevices, watching silently. They bowed as I moved further into the foyer. The flames thinned, stretching taller, thinner—as if straining not to be extinguished.

My gaze swept over the scene laid bare before me. Debauched decadence displayed openly: eight humans, arranged in obscene postures, bound and helpless, their lives dripping slowly away into tubes. Two were already drained, their lifeless forms sagging in silent submission. The remaining six trembled and wept feebly, prey awaiting the cruel certainty of their end. The mortals smelled of terror and arousal—a nauseating blend of survival instinct and humiliation. They did not yet understand that they were background decoration to something far older than their suffering.

But it was the five vampires at the table who captured my attention. Their indulgent display of carnality was both repulsive and intriguing. Naked and blood-smeared, they were unaware of my presence, engrossed fully in their own perverse revelry. The whelp I sought straddled the lap of a long white-haired male. Her head lolled back, eyes closed, lost in the blissful ignorance of ecstasy. A dark-haired vampire watched intently, stroking himself lazily as he claimed another female with his free hand. His golden eyes glittered with predatory lust. A third male, grotesque in nature, observed eagerly, touching himself, oblivious to the looming threat—now standing mere feet away. I knew them all…intimately.

I watched as my brother and the whelp's sire walked away from the table, while the white-haired female tended to her. They were speaking in hurried, furious whispers. At the mention of shadows and a single name from my brother's lips, I halted. Malevolent joy began coursing through me at her name.

"Dora…"

My voice, a low, chilling rasp, sliced through their disgusting festivities. "It seems I missed the beginning of the party."

The allure of the scene shattered in an instant, as five sets of eyes snapped toward me. Their shock and fear was palpable in their frozen forms. Lips pulled back into feral snarls and fangs gleamed in warning, though their bodies recoiled knowing they were in the presence of an apex. The music did not stop. It fractured. Notes bent out of harmony and dissolved into a ringing undertone. Every creature in the room felt it, even if they did not understand what they were feeling.

Recognition flashed first in my brother's eyes, followed by the whelp's sire. Their features twisted in undisguised horror, pupils dilating rapidly, betraying their panic as the others surged to their feet. I savored their terror, knowing the legends about me paled in comparison to the reality. Predators themselves: yet in my presence reduced to prey.

The white-haired female—Iyzebel—released a wild, manic laugh. Its shrillness betrayed her hysteria as realization crashed over her like a wave. She stepped back, her bravado crumbling, eyes darting in desperation for escape routes that did not exist.

I moved forward slowly, savoring every flinch and recoil my presence provoked. Shades gathered at my heels, flowing outward like ink spilled into water. Vakor stepped in front of the trembling whelp in a laughable, futile gesture of protection. Abbadon, my brother, stood stiff with false defiance, folding his arms across his broad chest. Yet his gaze flickered with uncertainty, revealing his own unease in my presence.

The room held its collective breath, suspended on the knife's edge of dread, until finally, the vampires—Vakor, Iyzebel, and Abbadon—spoke my name in a collective, fearful whisper, reverberating softly off the stone walls.

"Azvameth…"

The name sank, without echo, a weight so heavy, even the stone itself seemed reluctant to carry it. Their voices trembled with terror, feeding me. My lips curled slowly into a smile—a cold, pitiless expression devoid of comfort. I basked in their fear, savored their recognition of the ancient, primal darkness that had entered their sanctuary.

Yes, they knew me—Azvameth. The first, the darkest, the nightmare incarnate. Beneath their fear, beneath their rage, beneath their fragile defiance, they remembered. They remembered the effects of the first war. They remembered its ending and what came from it. And they understood…this was not an intrusion.

It was a reckoning.

Chapter 18

Azvameth

"Vakor… Iyzebel… Abbadon," I spoke their names, savoring the flicker of unease that rippled through each. My voice seeped into their consciousness like poison. "It has been far too many years."

Vakor's gaze darkened immediately, with carefully restrained fury. "How did you find us, Azvameth?" he demanded, voice steady even as his discomfort bled through the edges.

"Your whelp made quite the mess," I taunted, my tone sharp enough to draw blood. I turned my attention to the trembling whelp behind Vakor. My gaze held her imprisoned beneath its weight.

Kallea. I silently tasted her name, rolling it over my tongue. Such innocence, such fragile beauty, all hiding an unexplored darkness. Her violet eyes met mine—bright, defiant, yet utterly helpless beneath my gaze. Her fear radiated outward, intoxicating and deliciously tempting. Her body yielded, even as her will tried to hold her back, stepping cautiously out from behind her protector, drawn toward me like a moth to flame.

Black lines danced through her veins, so quickly that a single blink would take the sight away. The shades stayed just out of reach, as though debating on how to approach her. They recognized her…loved her…wanted her. They told me her name, and they told me of their desire. I only commanded them…for now…until their true mistress returned.

My lips curled into a wicked smile as she approached, her gaze never leaving mine, delicate fingers reaching out hesitantly. When she touched my chest, she shuddered. Beneath the simple black shirt, my skin was like polished obsidian, hot and unyielding, hiding a strength beyond her comprehension. I felt the faint quiver in her fingertips as they traced the sculpted lines of my muscles. Her lingering humanity, fragile and fleeting, fascinated me as much as it repulsed me.

"Your name, little one," I demanded, seizing her chin in an unbreakable grip, forcing her eyes upward. Her irises shimmered with terror, reflecting the endless abyss within my own gaze—void of humanity, warmth, or mercy. My eyes swallowed every flicker of resistance, every last fragment of defiance within her. A small smile tugged at my lips as I saw the black veins twirling in the vibrant pools.

"Kallea," she whispered involuntarily, her voice trembling like a frightened animal caught in a predator's trap.

"Ka…lee…a," I repeated, tasting each syllable. "Tell me… do you fear death? Do you hate the one who did this to you?" The word "hate" slithered from my lips, thick with venom.

Her eyes widened, pupils dilating sharply, her breath hitching. She struggled against my compulsion, desperate to retain control, but the word slipped helplessly from her lips. "No."

Delightful.

The panic surging through her veins quickened my pulse. She wished desperately to flee, to scream, to fight, but I effortlessly held her, my darkness tightening around her like a silken noose. Her fear was exquisite, a decadent nectar sweeter than blood. She knew instinctively she was in the presence of something far beyond mere vampirism—something ancient, primal, an evil beyond redemption.

"Azvameth, release my child. You hold no dominion here. Crawl back into whatever pit spat you out." Vakor sniped, his protectiveness of the whelp bleeding through each word, weakening the force of his demand.

His defiance amused me. How fragile it was, how feeble his anger when set against my ancient wrath. I laughed, the deep rumble vibrating through my body, adding to the whelp's own tremors.

"Oh, Vakor," I sneered, the air thickening around me as shadows writhed at my feet, swelling and collapsing like waves of dark smoke. "If I didn't know better, I might think you harbor some misplaced affection for this whelp."

Not hiding the contempt in my voice, I let it stab at him. "No, Vakor. I do not believe I will be doing any of what you just demanded. We may share half an origin, but we are not the same. We never were. She bore us both, true, but that is our only commonality."

I lowered my voice, leaning closer until Kallea felt my breath, scalding and deadly, ghosted against her ear. "I am darkness incarnate. I am the abyss from which your kind was born—the nightmare haunting your strongest kindred's dreams. You, little whelp, bear only the faintest echo of our lineage, tainted by pathetic human frailty. Yet there is something… something that should not exist, just beneath the surface."

I watched, fascinated, as the black streaks in her irises wove through the vibrant violet, giving them a living marbled pattern. My voice enveloped her, hypnotic and cruelly intimate, forcing her hands to rise of their own accord. Her trembling fingertips traced hesitantly over my chest, moving upward to brush against my lips. I parted them slightly, the tip of my serpent's tongue wetting her thumb, tasting her fear. My razored teeth flashed white, pointed fangs glinting dangerously in the low light.

"What is it you want, demon?" Vakor's voice sliced through our twisted dance, breaking the trance that held Kallea captive. She jolted, panic clawing its way back into her eyes. A twisted smirk curled my lips as her futile struggles ignited my predatory instincts. The way her soft hands pushed and slapped my chest did nothing more than leave light flutters in their wake.

Demon. Ah, there it was—the pathetic label humans clung to when faced with what they could not comprehend, a name that fell woefully short of my true nature. She realized it now, saw clearly what I was—what held her captive. Her voice broke in a desperate plea, trembling on the edge of panic, colored with rage and fear. "Let me go!"

I tightened my grip around her waist, deceptively gentle, yet absolute in its strength. Shadows surged around us, the black tendrils caressing her skin, binding her irrevocably to me. Her terror intensified, crimson and black rings blooming around the edges of her pupils. Desperation fueled her struggles.

Vakor's fear mirrored hers. He hid it well, yet it radiated from him like heat. He understood exactly what had entered his domain: an ancient, unstoppable force of corruption and ruin. I smiled darkly at him, savoring every ounce of his dread.

"You wish to understand what I truly am?" I whispered into Kallea's ear, my voice a velvety promise laced with cruelty. "I am older than your concept of time, darker than your wildest nightmare. I am Azvameth—shadow made flesh, fear incarnate, death's eternal companion."

My voice softened further, cruelly intimate, my words penetrating deep into the marrow of her being. "And you, little Kallea, will come to know exactly what that means."

I released her abruptly and stepped back into the swirling shadows, allowing their darkness to swallow me whole. Only the lingering echo of my presence remained—a cold, merciless promise that I would return. The vortex of shadows dissipated around her, leaving her weakened and dazed.

The shades took the moment to lunge. Flooding her nostrils and opened mouth, cascading in waves around her. As she collapsed, a sinister glee filled me, knowing when she awoke, I would see her reborn.

Chapter 19

Kallea

I was bound tightly to a rough wooden table. My arms stretched painfully to each side. Ankles strapped tight. A thick leather band wrapped around my throat. Cold air caressed my bare flesh, teasing and tormenting my nipples and the exposed, aching clit between my legs. My flesh was raw, hypersensitive—nerves twitched with dread. I tried to talk but no words would come. Dazed, struggling to think, the emotional torrent in me built until it threatened to break free.

What is happening? I want to go home.

In the distance, Vakor's laughter echoed mockingly, joined by Iyzebel's shrill giggles, the sound bouncing against stone like glass dropped from a height. The reverberation was a sinister chorus that sent icy tendrils of dread crawling down my spine. I felt his presence shifting around me, leaving waves of trepidation in his wake.

"They'll return, little whelp," Azvameth's voice emerged from the shadows beside me, rich and resonant, void of humanity yet brimming with promise. My blood chilled at the sinister undertone woven into every syllable. Even as the dark unknown within me trilled in delight at his proximity. I could feel its desire pulsing through my veins, calling him to me. The frigid touch of its presence caressing the edges of my mind.

"But first, let me share a story. Once you hear it, I will take you. I will show you pleasures beyond mortal imagining. You will belong wholly to me…for a moment…then you will be reborn as someone new. And together—we will complete what she began…."

He did not rush. That was the cruelty of it. The patience of something that knew time bent to its will.

A single, sharp nail traced upward from my ankle, drawing a thin line of fiery pain along my calf. I hissed, the agony increasing with each stroke under the weight of my fear. He traced higher, lingering briefly at the trembling flesh of my inner thigh. A whimper escaped me as I braced for worse. He circled his nail cruelly over my pubic bone, my navel, and between my heaving breasts, leaving cuts and pain in its wake.

Another nail joined in—then another—each deliberate incision opening my skin only for it to knit closed again, the cycle repeating with cold precision, as though he were mapping the limits of what I could endure. My screams tore from my throat as molten agony tore through every nerve, leaving me writhing, desperate for relief. Azvameth reveled in my suffering. His continued assault on my body drained what little remained of my sanity.

Make it stop. Please. I don't know if the words left my mouth or if they remained caged in my fractured mind.

"Did you worship God when you were human, Kallea?" His voice was calm with contempt, devoid of empathy, dripping venom. "Did you plead for forgiveness from the creator who abandoned you? Did you offer up your soul hoping for salvation from sins HE forced you to commit?"

Questions asked where answers were not meant to be spoken, no, they were meant to dismantle. His words cut deeper than his nails. I shook my head weakly, tears blurring my vision.

"Please…stop," I begged, my voice ragged and broken.

"Vakor!" I screamed in desperation, hoping the one claiming ownership over me would end this nightmare.

Azvameth's cold laughter pierced me as his nails ascended again, slicing deeply into my bottom lip, silencing pleas with fresh agony. *Please God, please make it stop. Who am I kidding. He won't save me. I am lost to Him. I am nothing to him. Nothing to this monster. Nothing to my sire.*

"Azvameth, stop toying with her," Vakor drawled lazily from somewhere nearby, disinterested, almost amused. "Tell your little tale and get on with it. Abbadon and Frederick have already retired, and Iyzebel is finishing her entertainment elsewhere."

Azvameth's gaze burned into me. His eyes were black. Not dark, black, as though his irises had devoured the concept of light.

"Please…why me?" The panic in my words fell on deaf ears. Why I begged was beyond me. I knew mercy would not come. I felt myself sinking deeper into my mind, willing the false safety of unconsciousness to return. When he spoke again, his voice was thick with bitterness.

"Millennia ago, God crafted two beings who straddled the line between angel and mortal—Adam and Lilith. They were his masterpieces, bound to please His whims and obey. And yet…He was merely a perverted voyeur, delighting in watching them rut like beasts. Eventually, Lilith defied His desires, demanding dominance."

As he spoke, his nail dug deeply into my side, spilling more of my blood. He brought his finger to his lips, savoring it. His smirk spoke of machinations I couldn't begin to understand but would eventually feel. Shadows danced around us, gleefully playing in the blood pooling around me, drinking it in. He continued, voice growing haunted, wrapped in wrath, and served with vengeance in its core.

"God grew tired. His pathetic ego bruised. Lucifer, enamored by Lilith's defiance and weary of God's petty games, rebelled. A great war erupted, tearing heaven asunder. Lucifer and his loyalists were cast into eternal darkness for their rebellion. The abyss you call Hell."

I had nothing more to give him. My screams left my throat raw and torn. Words would not release me. The bindings holding me did not give under my thrashing. I laid there, hopeless…waiting to break.

"Lilith was banished to darkness just outside of Lucifer's realm after God learned of her infidelity with the fallen angel. Ever the coward, He would not destroy His creations, despite His fury. So, Adam slept, Lilith vanished, forgotten, replaced by obedient Eve—until she, too, defied Him."

I could no longer see him. The edges of my vision grew hazy, tunneling until all I could focus on was a singular crack in the high ceiling. That single line, a taunt of the havoc it could wreak should it grow and give under the weight of the stone it held. I wanted to disappear into it. He took no notice of my glazed look, my weakened breaths, my frantic heart beats.

"Lilith's greatest revenge: carrying Adam's seed. Lucifer found her, sensed the dying parasite within, and offered her a choice: eternal bondage to death or immortality by his side. She made her choice. She laid with Lucifer, and from their union, arose the first dark Nephilim."

He paused, eyes ablaze with ancient cruelty and satisfaction. Before I could process his tale, he pinched my nipple with brute force. Flesh split and pulled beneath his grip, intentional, calculated.

Pain ripped through like wildfire, scorching me in its wake. My screams filled the chamber as he relished my agony. The depravity of his torture eclipsed everything. Then, he entered me, without ceremony, without tenderness, without even the pretense of desire. It was not passion. It was conquest.

I am going to die. Vakor won't stop him. I am alone.

His invasion laid me bare and his darkness spread within, scalding me from the inside out. The violence of his thrust, shredding me inside, the goal—to break me. My senses fractured. My sanity splintered. The pain was not singular, it multiplied, brutal, relentless. With a roar, he shuddered above me, pouring his dark essence into my broken body, marking me irrevocably. And worst of all, beneath the revulsion, beneath the humiliation, something in me responded. Not with love, not with want, but with recognition.

"…ME!" As the words erupted from his lips, he pressed his bleeding wrist to my mouth, I drank without thought. The force against my mouth splitting my lip. What flooded my mouth was not blood as I knew it. It tasted of sulfur, acrid and burning. My throat convulsed as I swallowed to avoid choking.

His declaration reverberated through my bones, raising goosebumps all over me. The cold truth sank deeper than his nails, deeper than his assault, deeper than the physical pain. Azvameth would be my savior, my grace—my death.

Everything felt muddied and disjointed, my mind no longer able to function. His words came in fragmented waves. Shadows swirled around me, caressing my skin. Their softness an illusion as every touch amplified the pain. They provided no comfort as I unraveled. Instead…they were *helping*?

His continued to defile me, seeking a second release, an ending to his show of dominance. The shadows twisted and twirled over my nipples, stroking my sensitive and eager clit, eliciting unbidden gasps of pleasure from me. Tingling started in my feet, shooting up my legs, then consumed me whole. The orgasm shattered my fear, releasing something inside me. My mind splintered and consciousness felt like sand in my fingers—slipping away.

"She is coming back."

"She is there"

"She is here"

"Mother…"

"Mistress…"

"Sister…"

Whispers surrounded me caressing my ears and pounding inside my skull. They moved in a frenzy at the edges of my sight, sliding over me, through me. They were everywhere, flooding my nostrils and open mouth, cascading in waves around me, leaving a burning sensation on and under my skin.

"Why…" I could not form the words. Thought was lost to me. Everything slowed. My body, heavy with the pressure building in me.

"You are the key to our return to power," Azvameth's whispered. "You are merely a vessel, holding onto a power you cannot comprehend, and tonight…you die."

His thrusts grew erratic as he reached his peak for a second time. His fangs grazed my nipple as he suckled like a newborn babe—his forked tongue flicking over the hardened peak. I could not stop the moans and cries that left my lips as another orgasm grew. It was not a release. It was a collapse, and this time, when I tipped over the edge, he followed. He roared, shaking the stone walls, dislodging pebbles that clattered against the floor.

A strange sensation started in my head, crawling outward, traveling along my body until every appendage was filled with the needling sensation. Then it began to morph into a raging fire that filled me—consuming the last vestiges of my mind. I no longer could think. Speak. Function. Darkness invaded me from the inside. My body fought the restraints as I twisted and struggled to break free from their hold.

My skin flushed red as inky black lines spread beneath it, tracing my veins and arteries. Buzzing filled my ears, muffling any sound—a steady white noise dragging its nails through my scalp. My own screams clawed at me as I struggled to form the pleas I wanted to speak.

"Make it STOP" The voice was not mine. It was the howl of a thousand voices in chorus, all sharing my pain. I thrashed in the bindings still holding me as the heat and pain intensified.

I felt myself dying. Was it my body or my mind—or both? My essence drained away, displaced by the slimy darkness slithering into its place. My body pregnant with shadow and evil, moving and kicking, taking over.

A void opened in me, drawing me to it, pulling me out of my mortal shell and into an internal war for survival. I did not want this life anymore. I wanted to go home. Home to my father, my mother, and my aunt. I wanted to go back to Anthony…my job…my education…to my mortal life.

"Azvameth, please…make it stop." My voice was weak, smothering my plea. I didn't even know what I was asking for, only that it had to end.

"It will stop. In due time, child, it will stop and when it does, you will be free from that piece of humanity you so strongly cling to." The inky black of his eyes stared into my own, revealing nothing.

My eyes grew heavy and my body limp with exhaustion. I felt the straps being removed from me and if it were not for Azvameth holding me, I would have hit the ground. I felt weightless as the room swayed, my vision hazed and speckles of dark spots blotted out the details.

Pain lanced my skull, sharp and sudden, another scream rupturing from me. I felt Azvameth's grip tighten, and as the black in my vision filled completely—I heard the voices again.

"She is her"

"She will live"

"Mistress home"

Chapter 20

Kallea

I felt myself lowered gently back into that cloud-like bed from before, its silk sheets now painfully soft against my raw, oversensitive flesh. Every nerve in my body screamed in agony as fire raced through my veins, each heartbeat driving the torment deeper. My muscles trembled violently, my skin slick with cold sweat yet burning from within as Azvameth's essence continued its relentless assault.

Fragments of memory flashed vividly through my semi-consciousness—Azvameth's body pressed brutally into mine. The icy darkness of his seed, invasive and scalding inside me. Him opening a vein. Forcing me to drink. It had seared my throat like molten metal, cascading liquid agony throughout my body, branding me from the inside out. I recalled distant screams, tortured cries—my own voice echoing from afar.

My vision had blurred red, a crimson curtain falling before everything faded into merciful blackness. But the reprieve didn't last. Hushed yet heated voices drifted toward me, penetrating the fog encasing my mind. Vakor's voice, tense with barely controlled rage, broke through the haze.

"Azvameth, what madness is this? Why reveal to her that you are Nephilim?" His voice was icy and sharp.

"Ten thousand years you've been absent, Azvameth. Ten thousand!" Vakor's voice trembled with rage. "Everywhere you walk, darkness and ruin follow. Your reckless hatred for humanity and *Him* nearly obliterated our kind once before. Why, after all this time, would you return now—and why did you give your blood to her?"

Azvameth's reply was chilling in its composure, patient…venomous. "Her humanity is a disease, Vakor—a weakness corrupting what should be perfection. My blood, the demon seed, will purge that taint. Once complete, she will be reborn."

"You cannot be serious. Reborn? I do not believe you. It cannot be possible."

Was that doubt I heard? Hesitance? What did Azvameth mean by his words? Does he know about the darkness in me?

Why won't my eyes open?

Why can I not move?

I felt his gaze on me even through my closed lids, his voice growing colder, harsher. "When Cain and Lilith birthed the Canaanites, it was not to coexist peacefully alongside God's flawed creatures. It was to annihilate them. Tell me, Vakor, do you even remember who you truly are? An original Canaanite, one of the first? How many of the originals have fallen since you abandoned your true nature? How many mortals have you toyed with? Feeding off their blood and their fragile pleasures. Playing meaningless games with Frederick and Iyzebel? Your childish antics diminish us all. My brother Abbadon belongs at my side. Not yours."

Azvameth's words sank deep, twisting inside me, reshaping everything I thought I knew about myself. Panic stirred beneath my immobilized body. Demon seed…his blood…my transformation— what was I becoming? My mind grasped desperately, refusing to surrender to the invading darkness even as it increased its pull.

My thoughts churned, chaotic… fragmented visions of my lost humanity clashed with Azvameth's sinister revelations.

Please God, forgive me.

Please let this end.

A strange thought…NO a voice…drifted through my mind…

"Humans and their blind faith in God—they cling desperately to that frail spark of angelic essence, foolishly believing it will save them. God had cast Lilith aside, stripping Adam down to mere shreds of his angelic nature, to control him, to bind him. Eve had been made weaker still, bound even more closely. Humanity worshipped a petty, vindictive deity. A puppet master who toyed with their lives. Who punished defiance without mercy. You will die, Kallea. And I will live"

Azvameth's presence loomed closer, thickening the air around me. His blood raging relentlessly through me. Its goal to purge and rewrite my very being, to force out the angelic residue left within me…making way for someone…*something*…to take over.

His voice dropped lower, quieter, as if sharing a secret only meant for me. "Humans, born with tainted essence, are marked at birth by a single drop of Nephilim blood. The angels' energy sustains our kind. Their essence, the purest form of life force, sweeter and richer than mere blood."

Brutal awareness crashed upon me, shifting my world irrevocably. Lilith and Cain became incarnations of lust and blood—the mother and father of vampires. Their progeny, my new kin, existed solely for these things. Creatures of the night driven by nothing but bloodlust and hollow pleasure.

Blood…

Lust…

Bound eternally together.

Azvameth's essence tightened its hold, obliterating the last traces of consciousness. Darkness embraced me like a cruel lover—cold, merciless, and utterly irresistible. His words sank deep, a dark promise reshaping my soul, burning through every fiber of me.

I was becoming something else. Something monstrous. Something magnificent.

What…even I did not know.

—Azvameth—

I could smell her, lying in wait, ready to be freed. My foolish brothers failed to see what this whelp meant for us. What she meant for us all. The shades knew and they covered her like a funeral shroud as she laid in the bed. Their excitement trilling through the air. I could hear them, talk to them, but only SHE could command them…and they wanted her home.

The whelp's body convulsed as my blood and the shadows coursed through her. Thick crimson ichor trickled from her ears, nose, eyes, mouth…every opening it could escape from. I knew the transformation would take time due to the strong will of the whelp. They would have to fight it out and the victor would gain control.

I trusted SHE would win and the whelp would fade away to the nothingness she spawned from. The wicked smile cut across my face, welcomed and unapologetic. Vakor paced with heavy, manic steps in front of the fireplace. His displeasure volleying off him in waves.

His affinity for the whelp unnatural for one as detached as him. There was no time for such frivolity. We had a family to rebuild. Kin to find. And a promise to fulfill…and she would be the one to set us back on task. My brothers may disagree but, I did not care. The old ways must return. We will rise. He will pay for His hypocrisy.

"Vakor. You will dig a hole with all the pacing. Do sit. I tire of the thudding. It is time and your accidental whelp was fate handing us the means."

"How? How can you act like this is nothing? Just another day in the chaos of Azvameth." His pitch reflected his panic. The volume rising with each word.

"Fate. You call this FATE? We are bound by law not to drink of the Nephilim. And, yet, you force your poison down the throat of a whelp! Fuck all. What is wrong with you?"

There was no suppressing the malevolent howl of laughter. What was wrong with me…what was wrong with him. With all of them. They, especially Vakor and Abbadon, act like they did not know what the whelp harbored. *Who* she harbored, locked inside, bound by light. Only to be freed by the darkness. They said her name. My brother and I were twins, yes, but he did not know. SHE was the true first. Born before us, sharing our womb. I have craved her ever since.

Even covered in shadow, the whelp was stunning. An eerie mirror image of HER. The color of blood gracing her hair. The vibrant violet of her eyes. Her soft, supple skin…all reminders of the deity that warmed my bed for thousands of years. Watching the shades caress her dormant vessel, proved I was right. And what a vessel…the only one worthy of HER.

"Do not hide behind righteous indignation. It is unbecoming. You and Abbadon knew what lay inside her. You are just too pathetic and diminished by your time with the vermin to see what I know. SHE will return and we will rise to be what we are to be." My gaze fell upon the shadow covered girl. They no longer moved, hushed and still— waiting for a command only SHE could give.

"We have searched for too long for the vessels Azvameth. They do not exist. They are lost and we have accepted that. You need to as well. This is why you were locked in Hell. This…" He paused as Kallea let out a wail with a thousand voices, as blood erupted from her mouth, a volcanic torrent staining the room with her becoming. "What. Is. Happening…"

His pallor turned green as the blood fountain ceased. Thick drips echoed through the room. Iron and sulfur scented the air, my comfort, marking this moment forever in time. The mortal shell of the whelp convulsing beneath the cover of darkness.

"Look at her! She is dying you fucking idiot. You will be lucky if this does not end with our destruction."

I smiled at Vakor. A true smile full of malice and joy. "It has started."

Chapter 21

Kallea

I was running.

My chest heaved, yet no breath escaped my parted lips—only emptiness filled my lungs. Beneath my feet, the ground felt soft, wet, squelching like it was drenched in blood. My footsteps echoed faintly, distant yet somehow close, as though another runner kept pace just beyond my sight. I glanced back, stumbling, seeing nothing. Just darkness and that sound, always just behind me.

Screams pierced the darkness—my voice merging with countless others into a chorus of agony and despair, a sound like an animal dying from torture. I couldn't tell where mine ended and theirs began. It all blended into a single, unending wail.

"Vakor...?"

"Izyebel...?"

"Anyone...can you hear me?" I shouted into the ether, instinctually knowing there would be no reply.

Darkness pressed in on me from all sides, heavy and suffocating. I felt hot—blistering and relentless heat—engulfing me in waves of scorching fire. Sweat traced burning trails down my skin, offering no relief.

How was there heat in nothing? Why am I sweating? Is this Azvameth's blood...defiling me from the inside out?

Far in the distance—a speck of pale, fragile light flickered, impossibly distant. I reached desperately for it, yearning for safety, for salvation, but it shrank further away, slipping between my fingers like a cruel illusion.

Why couldn't I catch it?

Did it not want me to get near?

Am I moving?

Why is everything black?

Laughter from behind me…or was it in front of me?

Feminine yet insidious.

Was I laughing… or was it the darkness?

Pain exploded within me, an agony unlike anything I'd ever experienced before. It seized my bones, my muscles, tearing through my veins with razor-sharp intent. My body arched helplessly, caught in the grip of whatever was happening to me. More screams wrenching from my raw throat, my entirety aching from the constant tension. I felt like I was being ripped away from myself.

The distant pale light turned red—a deep crimson as freshly spilled blood. A deafening roar filled my ears, like a river crashing over an endless cliff. It surged closer, faster than I could escape, swallowing me whole.

The red enveloped me, thick and warm. Shadows danced sinuously upon its surface, writhing and whispering my name. Their smoky fingers stretched out toward me, delicate yet irresistible, begging me to dance with them, to lose myself in their embrace. They caressed my skin, lifting me gently yet possessively, carrying me deeper into their velvet darkness.

When the wave stopped, I felt the sticky wetness of blood covering me. I coughed and wheezed, every breath a harder struggle than the one before and the pain was unending. Nothing made sense to me. I was trapped—trapped in an obelisk of my own madness. Had I finally lost it and my consciousness shut down?

Tears streamed down my face as hopelessness and the reality of my death sank in. I sank to my knees in this oblivion of my mind. I waited... for myself to wake, for someone or something to find me. Anything. Hoping and praying that this was not where and how I died. I sat... and sat... waiting.

I had no concept of time, though instinctually I knew I had been trapped here for a long while. Oddly, though I was feeling pain and emotions, I could not feel anything else. There was no longer a sense of hot or cold, just stillness. I felt like I was divided between two halves who desperately wanted to be whole, but neither side was willing to give in to the other.

I could hear whispers all around me, yet I saw no one, and no one spoke to me. The light had disappeared when the red wave came crashing into me. Was it my way out of this? I wished for its return, maybe if I believed I could grab it then I would be able to make it to it. Was the light my life...well, my vampire life? Was it a glimpse of my death? Maybe this was my purgatory.

Fuck, being trapped in your own head does some seriously trippy fuckery. How I knew I was trapped in my own head, wishing I would wake up was beyond me, yet...here I was, doing just that. Wrapping my arms around my knees, I rocked myself trying to soothe the anxiety clinging to me like my own skin. My body felt alien to me, I was an inside observer...just watching.

As if it could hear my silent pleas—the fragile light appeared, flickering weakly. Voices emerged from it, a gentle laughter morphing into anguished cries, growing softer, fading gradually as the shadows pulled me further away.

"Kallea… come back," the voice called to me, pleading softly from within the fading illumination—my voice, but not mine. I tried to stand, only to find my legs did not want to move and would not support my weight.

"Mom?" How am I hearing her? The light grew brighter…and closer… The voices coming from it becoming clearer.

"Kallea! Come back now." My mother's voice. Stern and sharp. The sound of a toddler's giggle fluttering from the depths of it.

"Come get me mommy." The little laugh. So pure and innocent. Now look at me. A monster…a dying one at that. The tears I thought were gone, poured forth. The memory of my mother's gentle patience a cruel taunt at the darkness I fought.

The bright orb shuddered and a new voice came through. My father's and the terror lacing it had me flinching.

"Kallea. What did you do? What did you do to Yaunnah?" I could hear the sorrow under the panic. My sister…she died in an accident when I was three. I don't remember this. Why don't I remember this?

"I not Kallea. Silly. I Dora." At the sound of that name, darkness rose to blot out the light. A frenzy of buzzing, anger pulsing from it. A laugh too deep for a child following behind them.

The shadows swarmed around me, hissing their promises.

"Stay with us…"

Stay.

Go back.

Stay.

Go back.

The two commands fought within me, pulling me violently in opposing directions. The light promised pain—sharp, undeniable, life-affirming anguish. The shadows whispered sweet relief, release from everything I had known, from everything human, from all suffering. All made worse by a memory I could not recall.

I had killed her. My parents lied to me. I was a monster even then…a child tainted by murderous impulses.

I longed for the light, I did not deserve.

I craved the dark. My mentor and friend for eternity.

I was trapped, poised precariously on a razor's edge between worlds. Each tugged at me relentlessly, both offering something I desperately needed…desired, both holding the power to break or remake me.

The shadows' voices grew more insistent, gentle and persuasive. "You are dead now, Kallea. Death has no pain, no suffering… only peace."

"I. am. NOT. DEAD." I screamed into the abyss. I was vampire…right? Pushing myself up with the last bit of strength I could pull, I started shuffling toward the light, my legs heavy and fighting every move.

I deserved to die. I had pushed my sister down those stairs. Yet, I wanted to live. I wanted to be everything Vakor wanted for me. I would push the last traces of mortality from my mind.

Just let me live…

The fragile, distant glow flared weakly one final time, offering exquisite, unbearable pain—the undeniable proof of existence. Was that light my human life's essence? Is that the 'angelic' spark the others so reviled?

Pain meant life… but I was no longer alive.

Peace meant death… but was I prepared to surrender?

I hovered there, suspended on the boundary of light and shadow, torn between torment and tranquility, between agony and oblivion, between everything and nothing. Sorrow and anguish over took me in an entirely different wave. I sank down sobbing uncontrollably as I continued the merry-go-round of thoughts.

I was dead…

I was nothing…

Yet somehow, I still felt everything.

I continued pushing myself to move faster toward the light, this time…it actually looked like it was getting closer. I felt hope and relief flood me at the thought of finally being free of this dungeon in my mind. I hated Vakor for what he did to me, even as I loved him for it. I hated Azvameth for putting me in this weird stasis and Abbadon for not stopping him. I hated them all. Only the thought of their deaths held the frayed ends of my sanity together.

Maybe I needed this so I could be a better embodiment of a vampire. Maybe they did me a favor and I was just being an ungrateful brat. Or maybe it was a toxic relationship that was gaslighting me into thinking anything about this was fucking okay.

"Hello little whelp." Her dulcet tone brushed over me, a soothing balm to my mind and body.

"Who are you?" I called, panic forming once again. "Why can't I see you?" My question echoed unanswered in emptiness.

"I am you," she replied smoothly. "You cannot see yourself, so how could you see me?" Her laugh sounded like shattering glass, sending sharp pain ricocheting through my skull.

If this was a dream, why could I feel everything so intensely? What was happening? Fuck…I felt myself slowing, my chest heaving from exertion, and my scattered thoughts overloading.

"Little whelp, this is no dream. You're dying. Your mind is desperately trying to keep your body alive—it cannot spare energy for mere dreams." Her tone shifted unpredictably from softness to menace.

"How are you me, if I am still here? What do you mean I am dying?" I demanded, fighting confusion.

"I've always been here. I tried before to reach you, but that interfering bitch bound me, preventing our communication." All softness evaporated from her voice, replaced by icy fury. I worried for the woman who did that. I feared for myself as the nagging feeling of my impending demise slithered through my mind, down my neck, flooding my body with the want to survive…my fight response kicking in.

Words in a language I did not recognize swirled around me. The fevered nature of them driving my panic further. At each utterance, pain stabbed at my head. I grabbed at my ears, willing the suffocating silence to return. Instead, more of that demonic laugh greeted me. The chanting barely registering under it.

"Show yourself!" I screamed into the blackness, spinning in circles trying to find the light again. I had to escape, yet no matter how far I ran or which direction...black was the only thing I could see. The flickering pale light slipping out of view each time I turned.

I could not move. Something about this other's presence kept me rooted in place. I felt the internal struggle between myself and her...our fight relegated to a battle of wills... and it would be to the death. Fuck her if she thought I would just lay down and let her win.

"Oh, I intend to—once you surrender completely." She spoke without laughter now, her voice filled solely with cold contempt.

"No..." It was the only word I could get out before I literally felt my heart being ripped from my chest. There was no pain, only the sickening, wet sound of tearing sinew, accompanied by bones cracking. I looked down to see my heart floating, still pulsing, still mine. The blip of light fading completely...in time with the beat...until there was nothing.

Huh...that is my hand...

"I win..."

Chapter 22
Shedim (Shades)

"We are one"

"We are all"

"We know all"

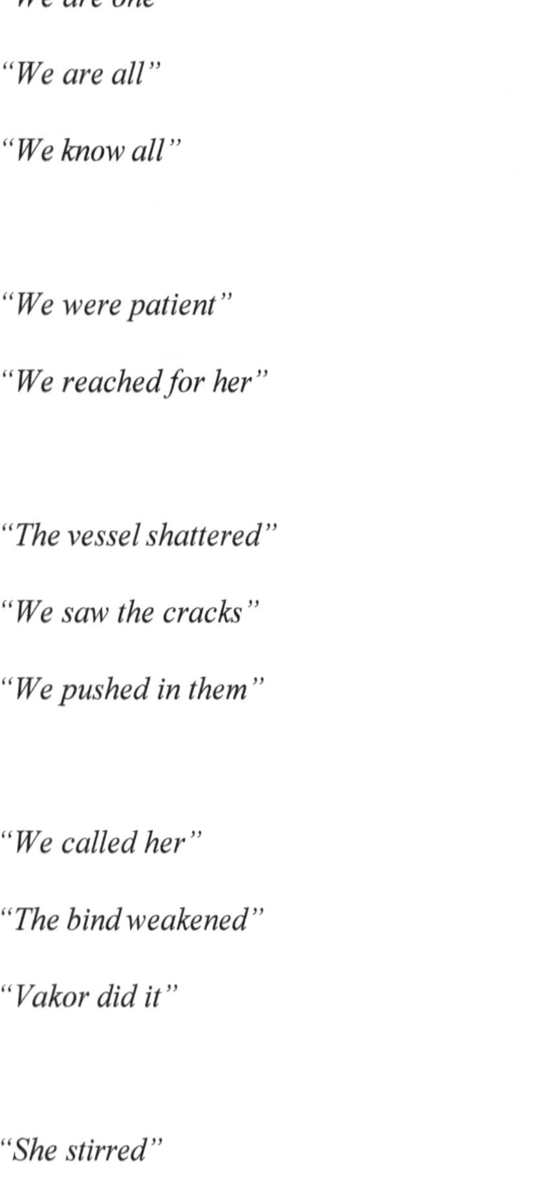

"We were patient"

"We reached for her"

"The vessel shattered"

"We saw the cracks"

"We pushed in them"

"We called her"

"The bind weakened"

"Vakor did it"

"She stirred"

"We called"

"Mistress"

"Queen"

"Sister"

"Mother"

"We hold her tight"

"We keep her safe"

"The human drank"

"Drank of the dark"

"She screamed"

"We rejoice"

"Nasty flesh die"

"Yes"

"Yes"

"YES"

"She stirs"

"Human dead"

"Mistress lives"

"We are the forgotten"

"The ones HE hate"

"Purgatory was cage"

"She freed us"

"She commands us"

"We are the first"

"Before the mortals"

"The first to be"

"HE created us"

"HE rejected us"

"She must know"

"The others"

"The statute"

"Betrayal"

"Vengeance ours"

"She wakes..."

Chapter 23

Vakor

I sat, silent and motionless, in the high-backed chair across from the bed in her room, my gaze fixed intently upon Kallea's still form. Days had bled into weeks, yet she remained trapped in this inexplicable sleep—an unsettling coma I couldn't fathom. Her body was unresponsive, but beneath her pale skin, shadows shifted, muscles twitched, twisting her into something I feared I would no longer recognize.

Behind me, the large fireplace crackled and popped staving off the room's chill. It wasn't the air that was cold, but a bone-deep chill no fire could melt. The curtains on the bed had been drawn back, allowing Kallea to be seen at all times. I wondered if she knew I was here.

It had been nearly two months since she fell into this state, this curse, this…whatever it is. No one could explain what was happening and Azvameth either did not know or was not willing to speak to it. Knowing that fucker, he did not want to speak to it, rather let us all be surprised…or mortified…probably both. And the shadows would not let any of us place an IV to give her blood. Blood that would strengthen her, sustain her, maybe even revive her.

He rarely came into this room even though this was his fucking mess. I had changed the sheets three times…soaked with blood she had vomited up between bone-rattling screams. The past few weeks though, she had been silent and eerily still. No screams, no vomit, just deathly quiescence.

It would not have been so unsettling, if I knew what was coming. Fear was not an emotion that frequented my mind, yet at this moment, it was all I knew. I hated the way it permeated my bones with its vibrations. Could the rumors be true?

Did the vessels actually live to adulthood this time?

It was no secret one of our brothers, a sister, and the first daughter had been stripped of their corporeal forms and were locked away. No one knew where or by whose hand. Over the myriads, we would learn of a vessel's birth, only for them to die before their first birthday. Some believed the vessels lacked the right lineage. Though, Abbadon and myself believed it was intentional…sabotage, to prevent their return.

I could not remember exactly what was required to wake their essence or how to free it. I remember something about *'what was born in dark shall be bound by light only to be broken by the original dark.'* The only catch was…who was the original dark? Was it Abbadon since he was conceived first or was it Azvameth since he was conceived after the fall of Lucifer and Lilith?

Could Kallea be a vessel? For too many years, we searched for our brother and sisters, and parents. We knew our siblings had been banished to vessels. We were just never fast enough to find them before the protectors did. We never knew how they always got to them first.

Fuck. Fuck. And triple fuck. I could kill him right now.

"Fuck… What is going on with you, pet?" I sighed, the weight of unease sinking into my bones.

Why wouldn't she wake?

Azvameth's blood coursed within her—a reckless, forbidden transgression. No Canaanite or vampire had ever tasted the blackened essence of the dark Nephilim. Not since our kind first emerged from the darkness—birthed by the cursed union of Lilith and Cain. It was taboo, an ancient boundary never meant to be crossed. Yet, that boundary now lay shattered by Azvameth's insidious meddling, his corrupted seed reshaping her from within.

I'd witnessed countless vampires succumb over the millennia, destroyed by humanity's sun—God's cruel punishment, His spiteful tool forged from angelic essence to eradicate everything spawned from Hell's shadowy pits. It was a brutal irony: God's wrath had forged us, and God's wrath threatened to end us.

But this transformation was different. Darker. More sinister. Utterly unpredictable. Fucking Azvameth. His recklessness knew no bounds. He did not earn the title "Harbinger of Chaos and Destruction" by accident.

My gaze lingered on Kallea, every change a glaring reminder that she was not mine anymore. Her fiery red hair gradually darkened, shifting into a blood-red so deep it bordered on black. Her alabaster skin, once flawless and smooth, now marbled grotesquely with shadows that writhed visibly beneath the surface. They followed her veins and arteries in mesmerizing synchronization.

Kallea was becoming something unknown—someone I deeply feared. Azvameth's cryptic words thrashed in my mind, rabid with possibilities too vast, too terrifying to accept. I was not ready to believe that after so many thousands of years, we had actually found our missing siblings.

Her arms jerked violently, muscles twitching as if battling an invisible force. My breath caught sharply as her delicate fingernails elongated, hardening into claws—predatory, unnatural, lethal. It was the first rapid change since the night Azvameth gave her his blood. The changes happened over the course of weeks before stopping abruptly, just like her screams. Until tonight.

Her face contorted silently as she struggled internally, trapped between two powerful forces. Her breathing quickened, her chest heaving as though she were frightened or in pain. Her lips parted slightly, revealing glimpses of razor-sharp teeth—her fangs longer, sharper, deadlier than anything in our Canaanite lineage. Whatever emerged from this transformation would not be vampire or Canaanite—it was ancient, dark, and far more dangerous.

No…it cannot be her…

Dread tightened its hold around my chest. She was caught between her dying vampire self and the dark rebirth Azvameth had forced upon her. I felt the fledgling-sire bond weaken, then vanish completely, a sharp, stabbing pain filling my chest as it died. I could no longer sense her emotions or her life. Inside, part of me wept while the rest of me brimmed with fascination and terrified curiosity. My body trembled with anxiety, betraying composure I tried to maintain. A single tear fell in grief for my pet, while I maintained my vigil.

Her eyes flew open—wide, feral, filled with anguish and fury. The scream erupting from her throat was unlike anything I had ever heard—a thousand tortured voices united in one bone-chilling shriek. The sound reverberated through the chamber, shattering my senses, sending daggers of pain deep into my skull.

I bolted upright, my hands clamping desperately over my ears in a futile attempt to block out the horrifying cacophony. The room trembled beneath the force of it. A shrill wail ripped at the fabric of my consciousness, blotting my vision with black spots. Pain sliced through me, sharp and blinding. When I finally drew my shaking hands away, fresh blood coated my fingers, dripping from ruptured eardrums.

Then came silence. Sweet. Haunting. Absolute.

Cautiously, my gaze returned to Kallea. She now sat upright, motionless yet brimming with an unnatural power. Her marbled skin was still, the shadows frozen beneath its surface as if awaiting her command. Her thick hair cascaded around her shoulders like a shroud, darker than spilled blood, woven from midnight.

But her eyes…

They met mine unflinchingly—dark violet irises now swimming in pools of absolute blackness. Shadows writhed hypnotically. Their tendrils swirled in mesmerizing patterns. An endless abyss, reflecting something older and more malevolent than anything I'd faced in countless centuries.

She blinked once, tilting her head with eerie composure. Her voice emerged from her lips in a quiet whisper, layered with shadows.

"Vakor…"

My blood froze as I stared into those unrecognizable eyes. Realization struck with cold certainty—Kallea was gone. In her place stood something ancient, powerful, terrifying—an entity of pure darkness. *Her*…

"Kallea…?" Her name left my lips as a question…one I already knew the answer to. My ears still rang from her screams moments before, my vision swam as I fought to clear my mind.

"No…"

—Dora—

The archaic bedroom felt foreign to me. It was clear I was in a vastly different time from when I had been banished to flesh. Vakor stood looking at me with his eyes wide and mouth hanging open. Pathetic. Then to have the audacity to call me by that disgusting creature's name, it was insulting at best. I stretched, feeling muscles and tendons loosen, and my shades purred at the movement.

I held my hand out to them and they twined eagerly around my fingers—an embrace of reverence and affection. It had been too long since I touched them, talked to them, used them.

I opened my mind to them. Only a gentle tone, what little my black heart allowed, could reach them. Too harsh and they splintered, their voices lost. They could never string together more than a few words at once. Yet, they were always a wealth of information and could find anything out…anywhere.

"Hello, my loves."

"Mistress."

"Mother."

"You return."

"Yes, my children. I return."

"We knew."

"Azvameth knew."

"Abbadon feared."

"Vakor feared."

"We celebrate."

"Tell me… do we know who bound me?"

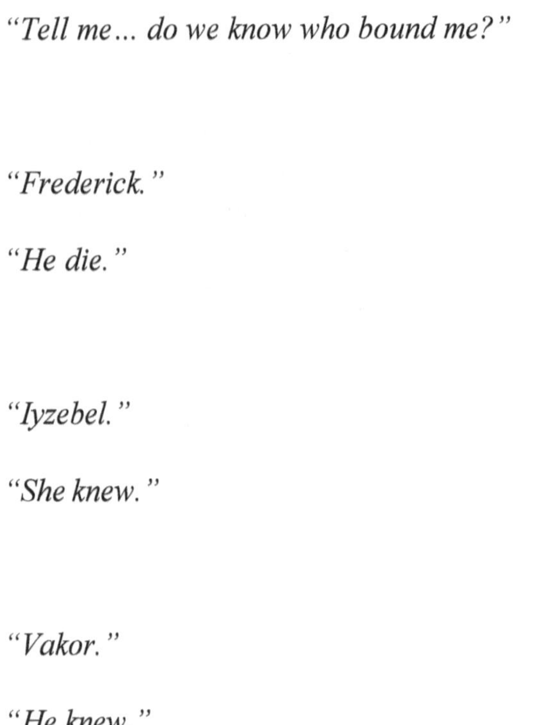

"Frederick."

"He die."

"Iyzebel."

"She knew."

"Vakor."

"He knew."

I fixed my gaze on my brother, narrowing my eyes. He knew I had been bound inside this human and he did nothing. My fury rippled through my dark children. A few darted toward Vakor's feet, but I called them back with a single command.

"No my children. His penitence will be paid to me."

Chapter 24

Abbadon

"What have you done, Azvameth?" My voice thundered through the cavernous chamber, echoing harshly off the ancient stone walls. Fury blazed through me, hot and destructive. The great room, now empty of tables and mortals, lay silent yet alive with restless shadows held at bay only by flickering candlelight along the edges and the chandelier suspended at its heart.

I could not comprehend my brother's motives for returning now, after countless centuries, deliberately unsettling the fragile equilibrium we maintained. Though our mother had bound us from conception, sharing her womb, our fathers' essences divided us irrevocably. Adam had sired me, gifting me remnants of angelic purity, later corrupted by Lucifer's dark revival.

Azvameth was altogether different: born of Lucifer's wrath and shadow, untouched by any fragment of divine grace. Though brothers, we were opposites in every way. I had been shaped from lingering angelic light, yet raised in darkness. He, however, was conceived of essence tainted by God's vindictiveness and Lucifer's insatiable fury. Light and Dark Nephilim, two sides of an endless war.

I had retained traces of my sire's angelic purity, creating a strange balance of dark and light. Azvameth's essence was tainted due to Lucifer's fall from grace…rebellion echoing through every fiber of my brother's being. Darkness welcomed him, cherishing and nourishing him, granting him powers beyond any other Nephilim. The only one with more power was our eldest sister. She shared our mother's womb, but not our sires. No, she was sired by shadow itself, making her the true incarnation of darkness.

I paced across the stone floor, boots echoing like gunshots, frustration radiating from my every stride. My white hair fell stark against my shoulders, golden eyes burning with barely restrained emotion. My skin—ashen as desert sands—flushed faintly with rage.

Vakor had chosen this cave after the ancient war, the first war between angels and demons when continents still formed one landmass—Pangea, as humanity would later call it. It was a war before the fall, a war that raged mercilessly for centuries, ending only when humanity itself fell, lost to their own weaknesses. Even with it updated with modern technology, we still coveted candlelight for its subtlety. Rarely were the electric lights ever turned on.

The chamber served many functions… we fed, partied, met formally, and in some instances, slept within these hard walls. The vermin might have called it a multipurpose room, but for us, it was necessity. The second floor contained seven sleeping quarters for guests. Vakor's quarters were concealed behind the wall of this room. No one could access it but him, sealed by old blood magic. Only his blood could open the entrance…if you could find it.

Azvameth sat with disturbing calm upon a stone bench, lifting his gaze to meet mine. His expression was unreadable, yet filled with silent mockery. "Abbadon," he drawled lazily, shadows whispering from his very presence, "do sit down. You'll wear the stone away with your endless pacing. You've spent too many centuries guarding the gates of Hell, ensuring our imprisonment—mine included. You and my father both trapped me in darkness. But now, it's my time."

Anger surged in my chest, his arrogance rolling in waves off him— the calm before his chaos. "You bring destruction wherever you step, brother," I snarled. "Every action you take threatens the fragile peace we've preserved. You've been gone ten thousand years. Why return now—and why corrupt Kallea with your blood? What motive drove you to it, of all things?"

"She is Her vessel. You know this. You sensed it. I heard your conversation with Vakor." Truth…

"No. It cannot be true. No vessel has ever been found past the first year of life." Disbelief filled me. I knew he was truthful, for no lie ever left his lips. That was the thing about Lucifer. He graced all his progeny with the inability to lie.

Azvameth's mouth twitched, a ghost of a chilling smile tugging at his lips. His voice dropped lower, void of warmth, resonating with ancient malevolence. "Because, brother, it is time. You have been corrupted by your affinity with humans. You cling desperately to that pathetic spark of angelic essence within you, forgetting who you truly are. Your time among the vermin has weakened you—clouded your purpose. We are not meant to coexist. We were meant to dominate."

His eyes—pools of absolute darkness—swirled like living ink awakening after centuries of sleep. "Kallea," he pressed again, his voice almost tender, but hollow, emotionless…dead. "is the vessel who will carry our legacy forward. She will fulfill what our mother began when she chose…*you*."

Before I could respond, a piercing scream shattered the silence. It echoed violently through the chamber, shaking loose centuries of dust and debris, sending tremors deep into the cavern's foundations. My body tensed instinctively, muscles tightening in primal fear. My hands clapped over my ears as I tried to block out the shrill sound. Sticky wetness flooded my ear canals, spilling onto my hands.

I looked to Azvameth, and froze in horror. His reaction chilled me to my core: a thin smile spreading across his lips, never reaching his eyes, which glittered triumphantly. The shadows surrounding him surged to life, churning in violent celebration, fully awakened for the first time in ages.

"She is awake," Azvameth sneered. His tone was ancient evil made audible. Dread coiled within me. The uncertainty of what was next squeezed my heart like a vice. What had he awakened?

What was Kallea becoming?

Could she truly be the vessel harboring our sister, Dora?

I stood paralyzed. The lingering echo of her agonized scream still reverberated in my ears, twisting terror deep in my gut. My eyes met my brother's, and for the first time in ages, I felt genuine fear—fear of the unknown. Fear of Azvameth's true intentions. Fear for our kin.

He smiled again, broader now, darkness gathering at the corners of his grin. The shadows wrapped tightly around him, their hisses cooing with malice. "Now, brother," he whispered, his voice a promise of chaos and ruin, "the real war begins."

"What do you mean the real war begins?" I heard the male's voice before I saw him. Frederick strolled in, his nonchalance announcing his presence, catching Azvameth's last words. "Seriously though, Azvameth…could you not have waited until Iyzebel and I retired to our estate before unleashing—whatever it is you unleashed?"

Azvameth's jaw clenched at his flippant tone. Even the shadows bristled at the youngest Canaanite's intrusion. They hissed at his approach, causing him to pause and raise his hands in supplication. For all his bravado, even he knew how dangerously close to the precipice he was. The hostility was so thick, it tugged at the bloodlust coiled deep in me. And yet, the fool still wore his trademark grin, as if fear had never known his name.

Why were they acting like that toward him?

"Easy now Az, my dearest brother. No need to sic the minions on me. I know they are feeling a bit excitable with their mummy dearest coming back to them." His mocking laughter dug at my eardrums more than the anguished screams behind Kallea's bedroom door.

"Vakor still up there with her?" The question was too casual. He asked like he did not recognize the gravity of what was unfolding.

Azvameth rose from his spot, walking purposefully toward Frederick, his face set in malice. I watched him, with bated breath, afraid of what he would do to our youngest sibling. Frederick had just enough sense to bow his head in quiet submission. I feared the recognition of his error was too late.

"You think I care about your dalliance with the Jezebel of our kind or your peace? Iyzebel will fuck anything." Azvameth circled Frederick like a predator stalking its next kill. I watched Frederick's olive complexion paled ghost-white, the faintest of trembles visible in the fabric of his palazzo pants and the loose Henley shirt. "You would know what is happening to that whelp since you were the one who tried to kill her when she was a babe barely out of her mother's womb."

Before I could move, Azvameth's hand punched through the front of Frederick's chest. His fingers curled around the still beating heart. He dropped it to the floor, blood falling from his fingertips. Then he seized Frederick's head and tore it free like parchment. The body fell with a sickening thud, blood pooling from the exposed neck. Dropping the head, Azvameth turned to me, his smile all razors and demonic.

"Now…shall we go greet our sister?" His hollow laugh trailed behind him as he walked away, licking his fingers.

I gave one last look at our brother, and sighed.

Hell of a way to start a family reunion…

Chapter 25

Vakor

Her eyes.

Once captivating and perfectly violet, they now floated eerily in a sea of shifting shadows. No whites remained—only endless darkness pooling around her glowing irises. Her lips had darkened too, becoming as rich and deep as her newly blood-red hair. Kallea was becoming something beyond my comprehension, beyond control, and for the first time in countless millennia, fear clawed its way into my chest.

Untouched by fear, I had existed as long as humanity itself, witnessing civilizations rise and crumble—unshakable and invulnerable. Yet now, standing before her transformed form, I realized there were only two beings who had every truly unnerved me: Azvameth and the creature Kallea was becoming…my sister…*Dora*.

"Kallea…" My voice caught in my throat as her head whipped toward me. I stared helplessly into those eyes, unable to break free. They pulled at something ancient and primal, a dark net of shadows, winding deeper into me. *No, not Kallea. I know this. And yet…I cannot reconcile it.*

Her voice drifted toward me, colder than ice, layered with the echo of countless whispers. "Vakor," she said, the word simultaneously seductive and chilling. "Earlier you mentioned settling the fleshbag's affairs when you visited Anthony and Amber. Let *us* take care of that now."

A shiver ran down my spine, but I forced a composed nod. "I already have Tuttle here with the papers and your accounts have been moved." Not her's…No. They where Pet's accounts…were…past tense. She was gone.

"Very well," she replied softly, her voice edged with amusement—a dark, twisted amusement out of place for one so young. With movements as fluid as the shadows that surrounded her, she crossed to the bureau and pulled out a pair of tight, dark jeans and a sleek black crop top. The disturbing marbling in her skin faded, returning to flawless porcelain. I quickly realized it was only a mask, concealing the dark truth writhing within her.

I could not tear my eyes away. My pulse quickened as I watched her dress, every line of her body calling to something primal within me. Uncontrollable desire surged through me, aching and undeniable. I hardened, her lust radiating in waves that crashed over me. As if sensing my need, she chuckled—a chillingly seductive sound resonating deep within my bones.

Before I could react, she was upon me. She slammed into me with surprising strength, moving me with little effort toward the bed. Shadows danced in her gaze, dangerous and alluring. They drew me further into her web, daring me to surrender.

Her lips captured mine in a violent, ravenous kiss. My bottom lip tore open under her teeth as her tongue drove deep, tasting me with feral intent. Lust and fear clashed, one demanding my surrender, the other screaming to flee. I wrapped my arms around her, lifting her onto the bed, her lithe body light in my grasp. But the instant I laid her down, she laughed. The sound—confident, laced with warning—like she knew my secrets. She flipped us with shocking ease, pinning me beneath her. Her strength had more than doubled—unnatural and intoxicating, pulling a hungry snarl from me.

Breathless, I stared up at her, enraptured by her supple breasts and the alluring path downward to the velvet heat between her thighs. The way her skin glowed with an inner radiance had me painfully aching to be buried deep in her. She lowered herself onto me. I felt exquisite silk envelop my cock as her muscles rippled powerfully, moving atop me with a rhythm that was fierce, brutal, dominating—each thrust a violent claim wrenching pleasure from me.

Unable to resist, I seized her nipples, pinching and pulling, each gasp fueling our lust-driven frenzy. She rode me with savagery and control, driving herself to the edge of release. Our pace quickened, hard and relentless, causing the heavy wood bed to groan under the assault.

Her head tilted back, dark hair brushing my legs, featherlight. The sensation sent ripples through my thighs, tightening low and deep— pooling in my balls, pushing me to the edge. As my climax surged, an insidious sensation arose—an undeniable drain on my very essence.

My eyes widened in shock. Shadows surged around us, passing through me into her, feeding her insatiable hunger. My ancient power bled away, pulled inexorably toward the darkness within Dora. When she looked down again, those haunting eyes had returned fully—violet rings set against infinite blackness, cold and bottomless.

Panic surged as my strength drained away. My muscles seized and every breath came harder than the last. "Dora…stop!" Azvameth's voice cut through the air, stopping her and the shadows.

She froze, the black in her eyes stilling as the shadows receded. A small, crooked smile twisted her darkened lips as she climbed gracefully off my weakened form, leaving me gasping desperately. My limbs were heavy, refusing to obey, no matter how hard I begged them.

"Dora…? Azvameth…what…did…you…do?" I choked out, panic and confusion lacing my weakened words. Our sister reborn…it explained so much and, yet, answered so little. We all knew Dora was trapped inside a human. I even knew Kallea could hear the shadows after she was turned. But in my arrogance, I dismissed the truth.

"Dora, please do not kill Vakor. As annoying as he may be to us, he is still our kin." I growled at the amusement in his voice, forcing my lungs to expand, willing the haze in my mind to clear.

"I would not dare to kill him. I simply needed some extra energy. We have a lot to prepare for…don't we, Azvameth." The way her hand moved down Azvameth's face was intimate, a lover's silent vow. I watched as they embraced, their kiss growing more feral with each moment.

"My children did not forget what he did to me. So let this serve as a warning." I did not miss the promise in her words. Her gaze silenced any retort before it could form.

She knows…

"Not…to…interrupt…" Coughing wracked my body as my lungs remembered how to function. "But I need to feed."

They both looked at me, whether with surprise or disgust, I did not care. I was pissed and barely hanging on to consciousness. She crossed the room without a backward glance, reclaiming the clothes she tossed aside mid-frenzy.

"I will not harm you again, brother. So long as you remember… I can and *will* end you should you betray me… again." Those words were a foreshadowing of my death. It was not an *if*… no it was a *when*. Dora never let the smallest slight against her pass. It always ended in death.

Abbadon gripped my shoulder and slung my arm over his. *When had he come in? How did I not feel him arrive?* He hefted me from the spot where I laid, holding me up as we made our way toward the bedroom door. Azvameth stepped aside to let us pass. Abbadon turned to him, silently communicating through that pointed stare.

Me…I watched as Dora moved across the stone floor, silent as a ghost, shadows swirling affectionately around her feet as she stepped out the door.

"Bring me Anthony and Amber."

She paused.

"And Iyzebel."

Chapter 26

Dora

My fingers wrapped firmly around the pen as I took it from Tuttle. His stubby sausage-like fingers brushed against mine, drawing a grimace to my lips. This simple transaction—securing Kallea's trust fund into a new account, under an alias, was a perfect means of revenge against her *father*. Each falsified document represented far more than mere legality; it was power shifting hands, wealth vanishing into offshore havens, guarded fiercely by our kind.

Across from me, Tuttle offered a forced smile, his clammy hand trembling as the pen left his grip. Even undead, his body carried the grotesque echoes of his human life, rolls of flesh heaving with every labored movement, slick hair plastered across a balding scalp. The sickly pallor of his skin did little to mask the terror emanating from him, pungent and intoxicating in its purity.

Shadows coiled sinuously around me, caressing my form with seductive familiarity, colder than ice yet infinitely comforting. I sensed the turmoil within Tuttle's mind, the frantic pulse of dread quickening despite his vampiric nature. He cleared his throat, voice wavering as he broke the charged silence. The tremble in his hand betrayed his composure as he reached for the papers.

"Well, Miss Moldovan, you are now in full control of everything. Vakor has settled my payment, so I will just—"

His words died as my lips curved upward, a dark, threatening smile playing across my features. Tuttle, in all his loathsome vulnerability, intrigued me—his terror like the sweetest aphrodisiac. The shades nipped at him, feeding from his heightened emotions.

From the depths of shadow, Azvameth and Abbadon watched in silence. Their ancient presence saturated the atmosphere, powerful and oppressive. I reveled in it. They may have been the original Nephilim, but they were nothing compared to me.

I was the *only* true immortal, born from shadow and Lilith, gifted by purgatory, God's little prison given breath and life. Their loyalty to me…unwavering…even through my past confinement. It granted me the ability to dissolve my form into the tiniest spaces light could not reach.

I leveled a look in Tuttle's direction, silently urging him to give in to the shadows so we could feed from him. His breath quickened, helpless before my unspoken command. His resistance unraveled thread by thread. He slouched in the chair, his eyes flickering between me and Vakor.

Vakor sat slumped nearby, his arrogant demeanor quickly beaten into submission, his powerful frame weakened and drained, his golden eyes dull from providing the sustenance I needed upon waking. The energy I took from him still coursed within me, fueling my malevolence.

This realization sent a fresh shiver of pleasure down my spine. Unlike my Canaanite kin, I did not require blood to sustain me. Fear, energy, and souls fed me. One person or a crowd, vampire, Canaanite, it made no difference—shadows were everywhere and they hunted and gathered essence for our mutual survival. I was the devourer of souls.

Panic rippled visibly through Tuttle, slamming the walls back down in his mind, severing my hold on him. His pudgy hands shook uncontrollably as he hastily gathered the remaining papers, nearly dropping them in his desperation to escape.

"I'll…be going now," he stammered, stumbling backward gracelessly, his large frame wobbling as he hurried away from me.

"Oh, and Tuttle, do not let me see you again." No elaboration was needed. My intent was clear.

My laughter followed him—a seductive melody woven with cruelty, a thousand voices layered with malice. It echoed in the air, resounding painfully in Tuttle's ears as he vanished into the corridor. I heard my brothers' grunts as they covered their ears. One of the perks of being me... I can and will make you bleed without ever touching you.

A moment later, screams erupted from the foyer—Anthony and Amber pleading, begging futilely for mercy, their fear saturating the air, potent and exhilarating. My laughter deepened, accompanied now by whispers of shadows joining in sinister harmony. Even Vakor flinched visibly, his grimace betraying his discomfort at the unnatural symphony resonating around us.

I was finally returned to my corporeal form. Kallea should have been strong enough to contain me, her bloodline tied to the protectors. Her mortality was her downfall. The binding was agony for both of us. I fought it for decades. I supposed I should be grateful. Her fragility made my takeover all the easier.

While she hated Vakor and Azvameth, I was thankful for their part in my ascension. If Vakor had not been so reckless as to turn Kallea, then I could have remained trapped, or worse, could have killed her trying to break free.

I shuddered at the lingering residue of Kallea's existence, knowing it would take time for me to draw its essence into my own. She was fully gone, though remnants remained in the form of her memories and emotional variance. The disgusting aspect of humans...love. I grimaced as that word left a stain in my mind.

"Brothers… I do believe our entertainment has arrived. I hope you saved room." This time my laughter was light and joyful…and of course…deadly.

Chapter 27

Anthony

I should have felt fear, waking in that unnatural darkness. But I didn't…and even that did not scare me. There was no caution, no anxiety, no hesitation—just an eerie, oppressive calm that seeped through my bones, numbing me like creeping frostbite, inch by merciless inch.

Then I saw her. She didn't merely exist in darkness—she embodied it. Shadows moved obediently around her. They whispered dark truths into her ear and caressed her flesh like devoted servants, woven from ancient nightmares. She moved with the darkness, with the shadows, as though they were one. The way they moved with her, around her, and through her—you would think they were born of her.

Her beauty defied all rational explanation, so ethereal and perfect it bordered on insanity. Her lips glistened—wet and wrong. And her hair—

It wasn't black.

It was deep, arterial crimson, the same sickly vibrant shade that spills from fresh, fatal wounds. It shone beneath pale moonlight, and when the breeze caught it, the strands didn't flutter—they writhed like serpents, alive and restless, hungry for their next meal.

When she spoke, her voice wrapped around me like a lullaby forged in shadow—a slow, irresistible curse filled with seduction and despair. It called to me and I wanted to go to her, without thought about my own wellbeing. Her presence commanded obedience and I would have done anything to gain her favor.

She was the whispered warning in the dark. The cautionary tale told to children to keep them safely indoors. She was the presence behind every creaking floorboard. The unseen menace that sent dogs howling in the night, the reason the moon fled fearfully behind clouds.

She was the monster hiding under the bed, in the closet, under the stairs, and in the dark alleyways.

She was a dark, silent promise.

She was death on two long legs.

And yet—I moved toward her willingly, hopelessly drawn, like a condemned soul pulled back toward something forbidden, sacred, and irrevocably damned. I wanted her darkness. Craved her sinister embrace. I wanted her to unmake me, consume me entirely, to take without giving.

I felt the menace flowing from her in a tsunami rush, nearly knocking me off my feet. Everything inside of me screamed danger…told me to run…and still I stood there. It was then I noticed the swirling around me. As my head turned to inspect the movement closer, two glowing dots appeared through them…

"I can see you…" she whispered and the words sliced through me like cold steel.

I jolted awake, breath seized, dragging air into my lungs as though I'd been holding my breath for too long. My body shuddered uncontrollably, drenched in cold sweat, icy chills slithering beneath my skin even as the oppressive heat suffocated me.

That damned dream felt excruciatingly real, each night a repetition of the last—her voice lingering, seeping like poison from the walls, whispering beneath the bed, waiting patiently. I closed my eyes, letting my lungs refill with air.

I dragged my hand down my face. She was gone. Dead. I'd made sure of that, though it was strange her car had been found with a body inside. It was not hers, but that of a good Samaritan who had likely pulled over to assess the crash. According to the police, the amount of blood found near her car suggested she couldn't have gone far before collapsing from blood loss.

To this day, nearly a year and a half later, the case has grown cold. Speculation swirled online about what might have happened to her. The most realistic blamed a political hit because of her father's international ties. The most fantastical—she was abducted by aliens.

While none of the above was true, it still left a bitter taste in my mouth knowing her body was never found, knowing she might still be out there. Maybe she had amnesia. Maybe she built a new life somewhere, with no memory of me or the one she left behind.

I'd slipped that sedative into her precious water bottle—the one she'd clung to obsessively like some pathetic security blanket. The timing had been perfect, seamless. She had smiled innocently at the valet moments before; never saw the danger. Never saw me coming.

Yet here she was, haunting my sleep, relentlessly returning. I knew it was her…it was the eyes. Every time I woke, it was to those glowing violet spots. I knew they were her eyes. Maybe she had actually died and was haunting me. If that was the case, then I needed a priest to exorcise my mind because I was about to lose it.

I sat up trembling despite the stifling heat. The woman beside me shifted peacefully in her sleep. A grating reminder of my attempts at normalcy, amplifying the irritation already eating at my nerves. I was over it.

Sure the sex was fantastic, way better than the vanilla shit I used to get from *her*, but Amber was just a means to an end. Her father had promised the trust to me shortly after she disappeared, said I was practically his son, even though she and I had never married.

Stumbling into the bathroom, the mirror struck me with the force of a physical blow. Not just the dark, bruised circles beneath my eyes—the mark of countless sleepless nights—but the scar. Thin, stark, vicious pink stretching ominously from below my ear to my jawline. Two months had passed, and I still had no memory of how it had happened. The gaping hole in that night terrified me more than I'd ever admit.

I remembered talking with my attorney that night, finalizing her affairs, getting the trust ready to be transferred to me. Then… blackness. Nothing. Just waking in pools of dried blood—my blood, crusted darkly across my pillow, sheets, staining everything around me.

Amber claimed she couldn't remember either, though she didn't have a mark on her. She insists we had gone out, had too much to drink, and that was why neither one of us remembered the night. Deep down, I knew that was not the truth, even as my mind said the same thing. It felt…wrong.

The ER doctor hadn't believed my story. Hell, neither did I. That missing sliver of time felt like someone had hollowed me out completely, stealing fragments of my very soul. He assumed I was in a bar fight and gave me a pamphlet for a 12-step program. The fucker thought I had a drinking problem because I supposedly blacked out drunk.

The splash of cold water on my face offered no lasting comfort. I splashed again, and again, desperate to drown her memory, to wash away her touch, her lingering voice, the dream's sinister residue. Water ran down my chest, off the edges of the vanity, and was splashed along the bottom of the mirror.

"Get your shit together Anthony. She is gone. You got what you wanted. You got the job, the money, and all the eager pussy you can dip into. Get your fucking shit together." I don't know what I expected from my reflection—some kind of release? A sign?

I just wanted her gone.

But she stayed stubbornly, cruelly close.

She should have been dead. Even as I told myself she was, I knew she wasn't. Not even my PI could find her. It was only a matter of when she would show back up. I'd kill her then, before anyone knew she had returned.

Suddenly, a noise rattled sharply behind the shower curtain, freezing my breath mid-throat. My gut clenched, the room tilting on its axis. The curtain swayed—slightly, impossibly, as though something behind it had moved. I had to still be dreaming…it was the only explanation. Except I knew I was awake and this was now a waking nightmare.

Then whispers—soft, insidious murmurs. Impossible.

My pulse thundered in my ears, dread crawling over my flesh. No. Enough. With a surge of terrified anger, I ripped back the curtain. I winced bracing for someone, or something, behind it. Nothing. Just shadows scattering like startled insects beneath harsh light. Still, the cold dread remained, burrowing deeper.

I staggered back to bed, exhausted yet unbearably tense. The clock glared at me: 3:20 a.m. Always the same damned hour. The time the police showed up at our door to inform me of the accident, the body, the blood, and that she was missing.

My head barely touched the pillow when I heard it—a sound, a scraping, dragging noise from inside the room. It sounded like it came from under the bed or Amber's side.

My eyes snapped open. Terror clawed up my spine. My limbs were frozen, unable to move—not numb, but burning, thousands of fiery needles piercing every inch of skin. It felt like something was slithering over my legs and arms.

I tried to scream. Silence trapped my voice, choking it deep in my throat.

Then I saw them.

The shadows—dark tendrils crawling with malicious intent up my arms, across my chest, wrapping tightly, mercilessly. They moved deliberately, black fingers fueled by hate, darkness given form. I felt it burn in every movement.

I turned my head, looking for Amber. She lay on her back, eyes wide, tears spilling down her face. The shadows had her too, silencing her screams, pinning her, except for the forced arch of her hips. Lifting my head to further assess the situation, I felt bile start to climb up from my stomach.

The shadows were moving in obscene rhythm between her legs. They were fucking her—not thrusting like a man. Not even close. They were entering her, exiting through the mattress beneath her. What the fuck…

Then *her* disembodied voice—soft, cruel, dripping with menace—rose from the darkness, tearing through my mind.

"Hello, Anthony…" She emerged from the shadows by the window.

Her eyes—those damned, terrifying eyes—burned into me. The darkness swallowed me whole. Her stare guiding the way.

Chapter 28

Anthony

My eyes flicked around the huge room. My heart raged beneath my ribs, pounding hard enough to bruise, each beat vibrating through my bones, threatening to crack. Shadows clung to every crevice like a second skin. The place was carved into the mountain's living stone—walls smooth as glass in some places, jagged and claw-marked in others. A tomb for things that had no right to exist, masked by elegance.

A place where secrets came to die.

And somewhere deep in my mind, a frigid reality burned: this was where I ended.

Sharp laughter struck my ears, a thousand voices in unison, cutting deep into my skull. Two wet pops and white heat seared down my neck. I staggered, clutching the sides of my head. My fingers came away slick, warm liquid creeping down my jawline in burning trails.

My gaze turned sideways toward Amber. Though she was close enough to touch, the distance felt impossibly far. Horror twisted her features. Her pupils were blown wide, terror carved into them. Behind her towered an inhuman figure, his hand clamped around her arm. His fingers dented deep into her skin, tiny rivulets of blood leaking from beneath them.

She mouthed something. I think she said my name, but there was no sound. Her throat strained, tendons bulging as she screamed into the void that had devoured my hearing.

She reached toward me. I wanted to go to her. I wanted to hold her. Apologize to her for…what, I do not know. I racked my mind trying to figure out a reason for this guilt, but nothing came. My heart stuttered at the sight of her suffering through my living nightmare.

"Anthony…"

A breathy whisper crept insidiously through my mind. Gentle and cool, yet razor-sharp, it sliced into me like a surgeon's scalpel. My eyelids drooped, weighted by something viscous and warm. Blood seeped from my tear ducts, blurring the world into pools of crimson.

I closed my eyes to alleviate the sting. Wet rivulets traced down my cheeks and over my lips. I licked them instinctively, the metallic tang flooding my mouth.

Agony surged through my skull—stronger this time. I doubled over as nausea twisted my gut violently. Spots pricked my vision as darkness crept along the edge. My lungs refused to inflate. My chest spasmed, back arched—nothing came. The burn in my ribs was a living thing. *I am going to die.*

"Oh, you're not going to die now," The voice was too close. Soft…comforting. "That wouldn't please me."

Air slammed back into me. Fast… cold… It scraped my throat raw and flooded my chest with icy fire. I doubled over, gasping, heaving as my entire body revolted.

Inhale…

Exhale…

Inhale…the smell of iron, old dust, and something faintly sweet filled my nose. My eyes watered from the pungent attack on my senses.

My gaze snapped sideways at the flicker in my peripheral.

A singular word tore through my mind...

NO.

She was there.

Kallea.

My mind refused to accept it. She should have been dead. Yet she stood before me, in the flesh. Her skin shone with an unearthly luminescence. She was different. Inhumanly so. Her stunning beauty warped by the malice burning in her stare. A stare that assured destruction…mine.

Her eyes—black as the new moon, the violet I knew now glowed with supernatural power and predatory menace. They swam with darkness, promising oblivion, death, and ruin. Looking into them felt like leaning over the abyss.

She tilted her head, almost shyly, as a smirk crept to her face.

"I'm sorry," she said sweetly. Her voice layered with echoes and whispers, blending together. "Where are my manners?"

Pain spiked in my skull. This time, it drove me to my knees, shockwaves radiating outward from the impact. My fingers clawed desperately at the back of my head, trying in vain to tear out the excruciating torment. Skin wept beneath my nails as I scraped harder and harder. It didn't matter…I was trapped.

I screamed—at least I thought I did—yet no sound was heard. My jaw and throat ached from the exertion. I heard nothing but her voice…and the whispers. Those icy whispers, drilling deeper, taking my mind with them.

Cold, powerful hands seized me, wrenching me violently upright, my legs dangling uselessly. Helplessly suspended, I struggled to see clearly through the crimson haze. Warm wetness dripped from my chin. I no longer knew if it was blood or sweat.

My head lolled back. I was greeted by the solid black orbs of another monster. His hair was black streaked with wisps of white. His skin was hard and dark as obsidian. His lips split into a jagged grin, teeth like razors, his forked tongue flicking across them.

"Boo." His voice, the voice of death.

Please don't let me die here. Not like this. Wake up, Anthony. Wake UP.

"Make no mistake, Anthony…" Her lips curved into a cruel smile. Her voice, velvet and venom, caressed my broken mind one last time. "…you will die."

And staring helplessly into those eyes, I knew—utterly, completely—I would.

The shadows pooled around her feet, small pieces brushing her calves. Not soft like smoke. Not hazy like shadow. It was thicker— alive—and they rolled outward from her entirety…reaching for me.

I tried to wrench away, yet the hands still held me tight. The first tendrils climbed my legs.

Cold—burning, painful cold—sank straight into my skin. The sensation did not stay where I was touched; it moved, worming beneath my flesh, slithering further up my body. Everything ached and my vision wavered.

Amber's scream finally reached me—muffled and distant, as though I was hearing it through earplugs. I jerked my head toward her. She was on her knees, hands clutching her face, blood streaming from between her fingers. Faster and faster it poured from her eyes…from her pores. Her screams dwindled as her body convulsed. Her spine arched backward until I heard the crack of bone.

I sank into myself as I watched her torment. There was nothing I could do. I was broken. Defeated. Worthless—unable to save her—unable to save myself. Had I done this to Kallea? Was this her revenge, her spirit risen to torment me?

Kallea moved in front of me. She was so close…too close. I felt the cold of the inky darkness moving through my skull, pulling something out of me. Invading my memories…tainting them with its threads, then pulling them away.

Images flickered inside my head, in a rapid, disjointed reel. I could hear my mother's voice, smell her perfume, my father's laughter, even Kallea's moans of pleasure were brought forward. Then…they were torn away like a piece of paper from a book. Gone before I could take them back.

"You belonged to her, Anthony." The words vibrated through my body…they were in me. "You always were…now you are mine."

As I tried to make sense of what she said, my vision went black. I could not see anything…then I saw *everything*.

Gone was the stone chamber…Amber…her…there was nothing but an endless expanse of shapes in the darkness. Faces, limbs, mouths opening and closing in silent screams…they surrounded me…reaching for me.

The pressure in my skull built until my nose bled. Warm streams ran over my lips, some slipping into my mouth. I couldn't move. Couldn't blink. Couldn't even think without causing the pressure to increase further.

My head was going to explode.

Her face hovered so close our noses nearly touched. Her eyes glowed, twin beacons in the swirling dark.

"Breathe," she whispered

I inhaled at her command. As air passed my lips, so did the darkness. Cold…alive…it was filling me.

The last thing I saw…razor sharp teeth showing between her lips in an evil smile.

"Oh Anthony. Can't have you passing out." The words coming out in a chuckle.

"Azvameth, do wake him please." I felt the darkness recede. My mind cleared as awareness crept back in. "Abbadon…leave her. She does not die now."

I am going to die…

"Yes…yes you will." That laugh, the calling card of my ruin.

Chapter 29

Anthony

"What…what are you?" My voice broke, pain stabbing through my skull with each word. Agony throbbed between my temples, scattering my thoughts. My vision blurred, eyes hot with blood, ears ringing with a shriek of torment.

"She is something we never knew existed," Azvameth answered lazily, his voice dripping dark amusement and reverence. Each syllable sliced through the muffled silence left by my shattered eardrums, like razors through numb flesh.

His tone filled me with sick dread. The words made no sense, yet the twisted awe in his voice froze my blood further. Abruptly, he released me from his cruel grip. A sharp crack filled the air as my body hit the stone floor. Bones in my legs and feet cracked in sharp pops. I cried out weakly from the jagged pain lancing through me. My useless limbs, unable to support me, tangled beneath as I collapsed.

"You see, Anthony, she is my sister—yet she was born of mortal blood. We share darkness and blood, yet even I cannot fathom the full depth of her beauty or her power." His reverence for her flowed through his words, yet something else was there… *lust? He called her sister yet he lusts after her.* Bile rose in my throat at the incest lacing his words.

Through the haze of pain, I watched as Azvameth stalked toward Kallea. The two of them together amplified the malevolence in the air. He positioned himself at her side, eyes drinking her in, lust—and pride—lacing his gaze.

Her skin shimmered faintly, as if shadows themselves were stitched beneath it, pulsing with slow, deliberate life. Her face was sharper now, cut from stone and void of humanity. Her voice was no longer flesh and breath, but something older. A sound that seemed forged from the bones of time, older than hell itself. She was not Kallea. No, she was a demon wearing Kallea's form.

"You tried to kill her, Anthony," she whispered, icy and certain. It echoed throughout the room…or maybe it rattled in my head on surround sound. "I remember it now. That night, she had dinner with her father. They spoke about business, donors, plans—remember? You left together. But she never made it home."

I no longer flinched at the pain; my mind had retreated behind shock and despair. Flashes of that night, from her view, flickered in my mind. I saw her drifting in and out of consciousness behind the wheel of her car. Her scream as the car left the road, down an embankment, smashing into a tree.

I felt the splintering of every bone upon impact. The bleeding in her abdomen pulsing in time with her heart. The ringing in her ears and pressure from the aneurysm forming. Smoke and ash stung my nose. Heat kissed and tormented my skin. I couldn't see anything through the fog, debris littering the hood and interior. It all felt real, not her pain, but mine. My mind trying to separate itself from my body's reaction.

I was there, while being here.

"Then Vakor found me, fed from me, and abandoned me," she continued bitterly. The shadows coiled tighter around her, as if in comfort. "Death, Anthony, is only as permanent as the puppet masters allow…"

She laughed—a chilling, cruel sound echoing endlessly off the cold stone walls—and turned, passing through the towering archway behind her.

"Bring them…" she commanded, with effortless authority.

Fresh agony surged as my feet dragged across the floor. The broken bones in my legs shrieked at the rough jerks. Azvameth's arms holding me up. I tried desperately to command them to stand, but they refused, hanging like lifeless weights. Shame merged with agony as I realized my bladder had given way, unnoticed in my torment. My soaked pants clung to my skin.

Panic surged within me. Where was Amber? She had been right beside me. Now, she was nowhere to be seen. My peripheral vision had vanished, narrowing into a dark tunnel. Frantically, I turned my head, spotting a blurred figure beside me. Abbadon—tall, impossibly powerful, terrifying in his calm. Amber's limp form hung helplessly over his shoulder, swaying with each measured step.

Abbadon glanced toward me, cold amusement filling his expression. "She's not dead, Anthony," he drawled. "She's awake. Completely aware—trapped inside her own helpless body. That's the beauty of being me, An…thon…NY."

With each drawn-out syllable of my name, fresh agony tore through me, blood surging anew down my cheeks. His voice was as sharp and deadly as hers.

Abbadon's voice sank lower, dripping with malevolent pleasure. "It's being able to do…this…"

I screamed as unseen blades sliced across my exposed flesh, welts erupting, weeping thin rivers of red down my arms and torso. My body shook violently with each cruel stroke. Fire and ice rocketed through my veins. My muscles seized and burned. My blood thickened under the relentless chill of death.

The confirmation of my death flashing in my mind like a neon sign. I don't know why I kept thinking it…questioning it when I knew it was reality.

"Kallea…please," I whispered, desperate, broken, begging. "You loved me. I loved you. Think…please…" My final word faded into silence as my body began to shut down, piece by piece.

My head drooped forward, darkness bleeding into my vision. My knees buckled. He released me from his hold and I hit the floor again with a brutal, resounding thud. Pain drifted into meaninglessness. Death approached eager and ready to collect.

But it wasn't the pain, or even death itself that terrified me most. They were predictable. It was the creatures before me that held my terror. I was living the nightmare of movies and books. And I prayed to wake from it or to lose myself in it. To numb the hurricane of emotions that whipped through me.

"I am not Kallea. She is dead, as you wished. I am Dora." It was the final, ruthless clarity in Kallea's shadow-filled eyes, staring down at me, void of humanity, void of mercy, void of love.

Tears flowed freely from me. I did not care how pathetic it looked. The tears, the piss-soaked pants, the whimpered pleas for relief—they were my only signs of life…of reality. I felt myself being hefted onto a hard table. Rough grabs pulling soft leather straps to hold me down. My head flopped over the edge, my world turning upside down. The cold wood permeating into my bones, offering me false relief from the heat of pain.

Though I could no longer see my captors, their other-worldly presence filled the space with a suffocating promise of violence. I could feel their movements ripple through the air, though no sound was heard. The occasional clink of the metal clips cutting through the silence.

"Ready, little insect." Not a question. A statement of fact, an announcement of the torture to come.

In that final moment, as shadows closed in, I knew with absolute certainty:

She was going to unmake me.

Chapter 30

Dora

I watched Anthony—her pathetic ex-fiancé—strapped naked to the cold wooden bench, trembling. Beside him, Amber—his vapid plaything—hung spread-eagle on a towering St. Andrew's cross, wrists and ankles bound, equally exposed. IV bags fed them, not out of mercy, but with the slow drip of prolonged suffering—keeping their hearts beating for my pleasure.

Looking at them, I felt nothing. No warmth. No affection. Only a cold detachment. With each passing moment, memories of her mortality faded, reduced to faint echoes, meaningless whispers drifting rapidly into oblivion.

Her humanity was dead. Only darkness and shadow remained, whispering enticingly, solidifying my rebirth. Kallea was no more— her body built for my essence. I was vast. Eternal. Meant to be feared.

Azvameth had called me sister. That single word resonated deeply within me, and I knew with absolute certainty he spoke the truth. The shadows surrounding us danced and whispered, delighting in our reunion. I felt the tether — primal, unbreakable — binding me to Azvameth, to Abbadon, to the path fate had wrapped around my throat.

Fate. A merciless puppeteer who spun sweetness or tragedy with the same indifferent hands. Bestowing happy endings dripping in nauseating joy or delivering tragedies steeped in malice. Nothing made sense—only the cruel certainty of my awakening.

My thoughts drifted back to that fateful night of my demise and subsequent rebirth. I recalled the dinner vividly—her parents, the hospital board, and the event planner, Izzy. A striking man, easily six feet tall, lithe and beautifully muscular. His eyes were captivating—

one crystal blue, the other ghostly white dotted with black freckles. Even then, he had pulled at something deeper than desire. I knew now it was no mere attraction, it was the first tug of destiny's snare. My *father* had sensed it as well.

My gaze cut to them, curiosity igniting fiercely. "Azvameth. Abbadon." My voice commanded their attention. "What do you know of the statue called One with the Shadows?"

Both brothers stiffened, eyes widening in unison—fear and intrigue mingled in their stares.

Azvameth spoke first, his voice filled with awe. "That cursed statue holds the essence of Lilith, Lucifer, and Cain."

I snarled at the mention of their names. Their desire to control Eden had been their downfall. She was my mother, yet there was no bond. I wanted her dead just as much as I wanted Lucifer and Cain's heads. But his words did not answer my question and I gave him a pointed look, commanding he continue.

"Forged in clay during the era of Pangea, just after Eden fell. It was created in a village hidden within mountains near what humans now call the Persian Gulf. A tribunal of women—the Protectors—guarded it vigilantly. Aided by archangels and cherubim who watched over their village."

My pulse quickened as I absorbed his words. "Essences. Explain." *Was this the fate that had trapped my siblings…and me?*

Abbadon's golden eyes flickered, wary. He continued in place of Azvameth. "Niahama—the tribe's spirit walker—had the power to move between realms, escorting souls to judgment. She alone had the strength to bind shadows, carrying them back to Hell. She created the statue in shadows, finished in light, bound with pure angelic essence.

When Lilith, Lucifer, and Cain attacked, Niahama stood alone with the statue, her spirit bridging both realms to seal their essences within. Her sacrifice locking it tight."

"The same as me." I had to know how that waste of power managed to trap beings wrought by *Him.*

"Nearly," Abbadon responded.

I observed the stark contrast between my brothers' reactions. Azvameth's black eyes danced gleefully with malevolence; Abbadon appeared deeply disturbed, unnerved. The fear emanating from him only heightened my curiosity further.

Closing my eyes, I reached out mentally to my children, the shadows, sending them forth into the world. Within moments their voices whispered eagerly in my mind:

"Mistress, we found it… It resides with him… Your mortal sire… Marcio… He senses us… No. Not mortal… Celestial… with the stain… He senses us… Samael… "

My eyes snapped open, shadows swirling furiously around me. I turned toward Vakor, my voice dark and commanding, the resonance of countless shadows vibrating through every word. "Vakor, bring me the one who played my father. Bring me Samael. He holds the statue. Feed first—you look pathetic, unworthy of the name Canaanite."

Vakor flinched at the weight of my command. My power surged as the last vestiges of Kallea's essence dissolved into me. Boundless power blazed the truth of who I was, saturating the room.

Azvameth's gaze met mine. A slow, knowing smile formed as recognition blossomed within me. "You remember now."

"Yes," I said, my tone thick with shadow. "Brothers, your sister Dora has returned." My smile did not reach my eyes—it was an absolute, a dark promise. I had returned, no longer a whelp, but the embodiment of shadow, sister of darkness and light, daughter of lust and shade.

I watched Vakor move reluctantly toward Anthony and Amber. With dark delight, he dragged his nails across their exposed flesh, leaving thin, bleeding lines. Malice curled over Vakor's emaciated features as terror rose sharply in Anthony's expression.

I stepped forward quietly, reminding Vakor that Anthony was mine alone to break—Amber was disposable, a mere plaything to be used as desired. "Drink from her, Vakor," I commanded, slicing a nail deeply across Amber's breast, inviting crimson trails of blood to spill down her pale skin. "Replenish yourself."

Vakor's nostrils flared as his predator instincts surged forth, his fangs elongating hungrily. He latched onto her with a guttural groan. Her moans turned into shrill, piercing screams. I watched in satisfaction as Vakor's pallid skin regained its luminescence. His hair shimmered anew. His eyes burned brightly again with predatory life.

"My sister," he gasped reverently, lips stained with her vitality "I thank you."

I stared at him coldly. Siblings we were, yet far from a traditional family. Human morality held no meaning for our kind. We indulged freely, without shame or hesitation, bonded by blood and darkness. If they dared to face their own lineage, they'd find themselves just as incestuous.

"Bring me Samael," I ordered firmly, my voice sharp and undeniable. "He knows the statue's location and where to find our missing siblings. After all, the fucker is a fallen angel…parading as one of the spawn."

My rage had begun to simmer beneath the surface. That fucking angel and his demon bitch, masquerading as family while I was locked away inside that human girl. He had to know I was there…why else would he have kept her.

"He owes answers, especially about why his adopted child carried my essence." My voice hardened dangerously, every syllable driving in the warning. "He is vital to what comes next—no harm is to come to him. None. Is. That. Clear?"

"Yes, sister," Vakor said quickly. "I swear it. Abbadon and I will bring him willingly."

I watched silently as Vakor and Abbadon left. The only indication of their departure was a sudden, chilling rush of air through the chamber's archway, then settled back into oppressive stillness.

I fixed my gaze upon Anthony, fangs elongating, anticipation swelling darkly within me. The mortal vessel's memories stirred faintly, fueling my hunger for vengeance.

"Now, Anthony," I murmured softly, shadows rising and wrapping like silk around me. "You have my undivided attention."

I laughed—a chorus of a thousand shadow voices mingling with mine, echoing cruelly off the stone walls. I stepped toward him— ready to claim my vengeance. His pale skin, graying as his terror grew. The sheer volume of energy wafting off of him stirred my children. They surged forward, coiling hungrily around the bench, waiting for my command to feed.

"P…pleeeezz…" His broken voice incoherent under the strain of his position and recent torment.

"Puhleeezzzz, what? Do you wish for this to end? Do you beg for death? That would be too good for you. She may be gone, but her desire for revenge…I keep that alive." I mocked his sniveling in each word. Taunting his emotions to flare, to feed me and my children. "So sweet. So raw. Mmmm, you are a treat."

"N…n…" His failed attempt to speak cut off by touch. A single nail traced his manhood, the core of his bravado, his body betraying his terror. Azvameth leaned in, licking the bounty that dripped from it.

"He tastes of rot." He spat, and I arched a brow. Azvameth wiped the back of his hand across his mouth. "He is spoiled, sister. No good will come from his blood."

"Then we drink of his energy. Go children, feed us." With that, Anthony was covered in a sheet of living shade. His aura pulsed through them, Azvameth, and me, adding to our own, quieting our hunger.

"My sister. My queen." Azvameth pulled me to him. His kiss was feral…deadly. "Shall we take the girl?"

"She is yours. Her energy is depleted. Abbadon broke her mind too soon." I sat at the table, watching my brother seize her backside as he defiled her. His savagery was an aphrodisiac, igniting my own lust. Her whimpers spicing the air with horror.

Azvameth will pay for his transgressions too…

Chapter 31

Vakor

I guided the Audi A6 along the winding mountain road, engine purring low, as headlights carved narrow ribbons of light through the dark, catching wet rock faces and twisted pines. The city's glittering sprawl flashed into view ahead—only to sink behind us as we slipped through, crossing to the far side of the valley.

My mind drifted to Marcio—Samael's vessel—and the first time we'd spoken in centuries. He'd called me in the dead of night; terror laced his voice. He knew the dangers of contacting our kind. He held too many ancient truths, dark secrets, and the inevitability bound to his bloodline.

That night had faded into the long stretch of years—until now. Until Dora. The memory sharpened like glass under my skin.

"Vakor, Yaunnah is dead. Kallea… Kallea killed her."

Disbelief gripped me. "How?" I demanded. "How could a toddler possibly kill her grown sister?"

Samael's reply was hollow, heavy with resignation. "It's her. Dora has found her vessel."

The chill I felt then, struck me now twenty-three years later. Dora reborn… My long-lost sister inhabiting the mortal Kallea. *How could I have forgotten?* And if she had returned, what of Allocer and Citha? Were they still trapped in artifacts, or had they found a suitable vessel?

"Speak, Vakor." Abbadon's deep voice cut through my thoughts, its weight filling the car. "I can feel your unease. I suspect we are of one mind on this."

I exhaled, tension rippling through my muscles. "Dora has returned. She seeks Allocer and Citha. Marcio holds the key to finding them—and the statue. She intends to rebuild our parents' army."

The weight of my words pressed down, frigid in my bones even as fire coursed through my blood. The thought of reuniting the original darkness exhilarated me, but the certainty of the devastation it would bring, tempered it.

Abbadon shifted, golden eyes glinting with deep contemplation. "Allocer," he said quietly, "is a nuisance, nothing more. He's always been a hedonist, content with blood and debauchery. But Citha…" His voice dropped to a dangerous register. "Citha's hatred for humanity eclipses even Azvameth's cruelty. If she reunites with Dora, humanity won't stand a chance."

His fear mirrored my own. Allocer was predictable, manageable. But Citha—her vendetta was ancient, and in her eyes, justified. The Protectors had imprisoned our parents' essences within that cursed statue, then bound Allocer, Dora, and Citha in artifacts scattered across the mortal world.

"What I don't understand," I murmured, half to myself, "is how they've clawed their way back from banishment. Shadows cannot inhabit mortal flesh unless the bloodline descends directly from our kind."

"It seems one of our brethren has been carrying on where Lilith left off." Abbadon growled. We both knew this did not bode well for humanity, nor for our kind. Too much evil without strength meant another flood.

"That… or they…" My words stopped as I felt like I was being watched.

Abbadon's eyes sharpened instantly, his voice laced with quiet menace. "Are you suggesting what I think, Vakor?"

I shook my head, choosing my words with care. "No. We've always seen humanity as vermin to be controlled or eliminated. But I grew complacent. When Dora chose Kallea, I dismissed it, believing we still had time."

Abbadon's gaze narrowed. "You knew Dora had chosen her, yet you allowed Marcio—a Protector's descendant—to raise our sister's vessel? What if he'd killed her?"

"He tried," I admitted, my tone strained with the memory. "The shadows defended her, scarring him from shoulder to fingertip. After that, he guarded her, desperate to suppress her darkness."

"You helped him bind her." It wasn't a question—it was an accusation.

"Dora's essence was too strong, overpowering Kallea's mortal spirit before she could mature. Yes, I helped, along with Frederick and Iyzebel. And I killed the old woman who performed the binding, ensuring she could never expose us."

The silence that followed was heavy, suffocating—acceptance settling between us. The war Lilith and Cain began with Lucifer was moving toward its inevitable end. Revenge would be ours, humanity's demise, certain.

My thoughts almost carried me past the wrought iron gates guarding the looming gothic mansion. I slowed sharply, stopping at the intercom—but before I could speak, the gates swung silently open. Of course, he had been expecting us.

We pulled to a stop at the foot of the front steps. Abbadon and I stepped from the car as the heavy doors opened, revealing Samael. His features were etched with fatigue, eyes shadowed from sleepless nights, his body taut under the weight of secrets.

"Vakor," His voice was grave, weighted by our presence. "Abbadon."

"Marcio," we replied in unison, the single word carrying everything unspoken.

He nodded, resignation in every line of his stance. "Come inside. Give me a moment, and then you can take me to my daughter."

A chill rippled through me. How had he known?

We followed him in silence, the shadows whispering as we passed—threads of ancient truths long kept, now restless, ready to surface.

"I expected this day to come." The defeat in his shoulders lent to the weight of his words. "My Illyana passed shortly after Kallea's disappearance. The only explanation…the reason you are here."

I swallowed at the melancholy in his tone. Illyana had been his wife for many years, knowing that her mortal husband no longer inhabited the body. She had been accepting of the archangel, Samael, and the babe he held in his arms, the night he showed up in her husband's flesh.

Marcio had been the doctor to deliver Kallea. His death attributed to a heart attack, but Samael knew it was Dora. Even in the mortal's infancy, Dora's malevolence was too strong to be contained. Everyone in that birthing room had died…the mother was the first to die. Marcio followed. Then the two nurses who attended her before she was placed in the orphanage. All so she could live.

Had Samael not found her, the nuns would have killed her. They spoke of curses and demons when they looked at her. Her tiny cries piercing everyone around her as she lay alone in darkness. He subdued Dora, forcing some of his own essence into Kallea, but it was not enough. Not when at 3-years-old, Dora woke again.

I stood frozen at the threshold, the weight of Samael's sorrow heavy in the air, halting my steps. Abbadon and Samael spoke in low tones, their words fading as I drifted into my own thoughts. If Abbadon knew that Marcio was actually the fallen archangel, he did not let on. Instead, he stood there, nodding his head as they talked. I did not pay attention to what they said until Samael's voice pulled me from my thoughts.

"So, do tell Vakor. Let me hear the reason from your lips, instead of my aching heart." I took a deep breath, walking further into the home.

"It's Dora"...

Chapter 32

Marcio/Samael

"Dora has claimed Kallea." I spoke the words with intent, my voice raw with grief and exhaustion. Just uttering them drained whatever strength remained within me, pushing my aging mortal body closer to collapse. The admission settled heavy, like ash after something sacred had burned. Even the thought of her name felt dangerous, let alone to speak it aloud, as though it might summon more than memory.

I had always known this day would come. From the moment I found her in the orphanage, bearing the shadow's mark, I knew she was a vessel. Dora—the shadow-born daughter of Lilith, fatherless, harboring only death in her heart. She had not cried like other infants. She watched. Even then her eyes had not searched for comfort. They searched for exits.

"She has indeed," Vakor replied, his voice uncharacteristically heavy, grim. "Unwittingly, I set the process in motion that night. I found her barely alive, nearly murdered by her pathetic fiancé's poison. Azvameth, though—he knew exactly who she was the moment he laid eyes upon her. He used his blood to finish the transformation."

My stomach churned violently at Vakor's revelation. Azvameth had returned; the most terrifying of the Nephilim walked this realm again. This meant only one thing: Allocer and Citha were not far behind, their return inevitable once their vessels had been identified. My old heart thudded painfully at the truth of it all. The house seemed to crowd inward around us. The walls, the floors, even the air itself felt thinner, as if the world understood what we were admitting and had begun to brace itself.

I drew a deep, weary breath. "Vakor, we've known each other through countless myriads, in every form I've inhabited. We've always maintained peace between us. But I fear what I must reveal now will shatter that fragile alliance." I lowered my head, heavy with the burden of inevitable loss. "I ask only to see my daughter once more, before my final breath."

The word daughter felt strange on my tongue. It was both truth and fallacy. I had never truly owned her. Only guarded her. I was her warden. A duty self-imposed by my own sense of honor. Or was it guilt. Guilt for turning my back on my creator, my brothers and sisters, my kind. No, I had made the right choice at the time. Lucifer's insistence that humanity was unworthy of the Creator and their eventual denial of him rang truth. Even now, he was right. So why did I fear what was to come when it was necessary?

"Marcio…" Vakor's voice was firm, knowing. "Or should I call you by your true name, Samael?"

I nodded, no longer able to hide behind the veil of secrecy. "Yes. Call me Samael. I am done hiding behind deception." My admission echoed through the large foyer, final and irrevocable. To speak my name was to acknowledge every unspoken truth and it hung between us like a blade unsheathed.

"Samael?" Abbadon's voice cut sharply through our conversation, his golden eyes narrowing in suspicion and surprise.

"Yes, Abbadon," I acknowledged him with a respectful bow of my head, recognizing the Lord of Demons in his true form. "Nephew, it's been a very long time."

His stare did not soften. It sharpened as blood remembers blood, and ours had never been clean. The secrets we shared would come out…one way or another.

"You have much explaining to do, Samael." Abbadon's voice was icy, laden with threat. "How long have you hidden among these humans? How could you possibly have anticipated this?"

I let out the breath I had been holding, dread pooling in my stomach. The truths I held were dangerous, and I knew the moment I laid eyes upon Dora's vessel—my daughter, Kallea—I would cease to exist. Dora would see to my end for helping the old crone bind her essence within my mortal child in a desperate attempt to stall her inevitable return. And perhaps I deserved it. I had bound her. I had suppressed her. I had chose light—however fractured—over shadow.

I remember the day Yaunnah died.

Kallea stood at the top of the stairs, no more than a babe of 3. Shadows swirled around her. The giggles of a thousand voices filled the air, the shades tickling her as they played. Yaunnah lay lifeless at the bottom of the stairs. Her body twisted grotesquely from the fall.

"Kallea! What have you done?" I shouted through the pain and the fear flooding my body as I realized Dora was pushing through the child's consciousness.

"I not Kal…lee…a, Sam.a.el. I Dora." Her sweet melodic voice tainted by shadow. She knew my name…it was not learned…it was remembered.

"Samael…?" My name spoken in question by Vakor pulled me from the memory. I shook my head, turning my eyes downward.

"Yes," I said quietly. "There are many questions that demand answers and much to explain. But first, let me bring Mazikeen. She needs to hear this. Dora too will undoubtedly want to listen."

Turning away, I left Vakor and Abbadon standing silently in the grand foyer. My footsteps echoed through the corridors as I headed to the library—Mazikeen's eternal sanctuary. Since our arrival in this mortal realm, she had developed a peculiar infatuation with all forms of human literature.

I found her lounging in a velvet chair; eyes narrowed with irritation at my interruption. She regarded me over the top of a thick, leather-bound tome, her mouth curling into a smile equal parts amusement and disdain.

"Samael," she drawled, mockery lacing my name, "to what do I owe the displeasure?"

"Vakor is here," I informed her quietly, "and he has Abbadon with him."

Mazikeen's eyes flashed angrily, lips curling in sardonicism as she slammed her book shut, discarding it carelessly onto the ornate table beside her. "Why are those two asshats darkening our doorstep?" Her sarcasm bit deep, venom dripping freely as her eyes rolled dramatically.

"Dora has fully claimed Kallea," I stated flatly. "They're here to bring us to her. They want answers—and they are demanding them."

Mazikeen scoffed, eyes narrowing, not hiding the contempt in her tone. "I have no intention of answering any questions from those pathetic brothers of mine. Nor will Dora get her claws on the statue. That fickle bitch would destroy it without a second thought, and we'd never return them to their rightful bodies. She's always despised Mother and the fools she entertained." She paused, casting me a mocking smirk. "Except you, of course… dearest uncle."

I arched a brow. Her laughter, dark and humorless, echoed softly in response. A taunting ripple through her slender throat.

"Maz, think carefully," I countered, appealing to her deepest desires. "We can go to her of our own accord…or we can wait for her to have us dragged there by the shades. What appeals more to you, *niece*?"

Her bravery mirrored the calculation in her gaze. She was not dismissing the dangers her sister presented, she was measuring it. And at the mention of the word shades, she knew what I meant. Dora did not need permission to collect what she considered hers. Even if ownership or permission was not given.

A brief flash of genuine interest sparked in her eyes, even as she maintained her sardonic façade. "Home does have its charms, especially with beaches and endless margaritas. Humans certainly know how to craft an indulgent drink, though their alcohol is pathetically weak."

She rose fluidly, deliberately brushing past me with calculated indifference, walking ahead toward the foyer, hips swaying arrogantly. Her laughter echoed sharply off the walls—a wicked, sarcastic melody that chilled my blood, even as it brought a grudging smile. Her posture spoke of her arrogance, her readiness lying in wait. She did not fear many things. Dora, however, was one of them.

We returned to the foyer where Vakor and Abbadon stood like statues by the doors, their ancient eyes fixed knowingly on us. I felt the weight of the moment deep within my soul. The revelation of my true identity—Samael—hung heavily between us, shifting alliances, awakening old grudges.

Soon, we would face Dora. She would demand answers, unleash her vengeance, and set events into motion that had slumbered for millennia.

As I crossed the threshold, dread pooled thickly in my stomach. Mazikeen paused beside me, eyes glittering as she regarded Vakor and Abbadon.

"Well, then," she purred sarcastically, "let's go greet my dear sister." The word sister was not said with familial tenderness. It was prophetic, final, and weight with recognition of impending battle.

I took a deep, shuddering breath, fully aware that soon I would gaze into Dora's shadow-filled eyes once again, and my final chapter would draw to a close. Her wrathful ways knew no kin, no friend—only foes. And I was first among her enemies, the one who bound her, the one who tried to cast her out of the mortal child. She knew this, even as a child she called me by my name. This reunion would be one of revenge, not welcome.

My head hung low as I followed them to the car. Mazikeen had come to me shortly after my wife's passing, her warnings of restless shadows foreshadowing this day. Though I knew Illyana was not truly my wife, I had come to love her over the time we were together. She loved Kallea as her own and that love was what helped bind Dora. For God's greatest gift, and His most powerful, was love.

And if Dora had her way…all love, all light, would burn.

Chapter 33

Abbadon

The air still carried the heaviness of Samael's confession as we rode back to Vakor's mansion. The weight of his name — spoken aloud after hiding it for so long — clung to the interior of the car like smoke.

Mazikeen sat in the back seat, completely engrossed in the frivolous pages of human literature. Her slender fingers turned the pages with exaggerated interest. Beside her, Samael stared silently out the window, his form hunched beneath the weight of exhaustion and inevitability. The scent radiating from him was a disturbing mix of regret and despair—strange in any being, but almost grotesque on a fallen archangel whose essence still pulsed faintly with angelic purity, even after his shadow-tainted fall from grace.

"Samael," I finally broke the suffocating silence. My irritation sharpened words, "why do you reek of mortal sentiment?"

His sudden intake of breath told me my strike had landed. He turned his head slowly toward me, the tension in his jaw evident. "I wouldn't expect you to understand," he replied, voice clipped and bitter, every word weighted with centuries of resentment.

Always brooding, always irritatingly pugnacious. He carried his emotions like a martyr, wrapped tightly in his own melancholy. Unlike him, I was not forged in the Creator's light. I had never been granted the dubious privilege of meeting our self-righteous progenitor—something I counted as a mercy. The Almighty—hypocrite, deceiver, tyrant—everything He accused Lucifer of being. All my father ever wanted was *equal adoration, equal worship* to what was freely given to these pathetic and unworthy mortals. For that, He condemned him to shadow.

"Try me," I snapped back sharply, my patience already frayed thin.

"Abbadon, enough." Vakor's voice sliced from the driver's seat, commanding yet weary. "Whatever Samael has to say can wait until we return home—to Dora."

That name hung between us, heavier than the quiet that followed. Dora. My mind flickered, unbidden, to the taste of her blood on my tongue—an electrifying jolt of recognition, though I was not certain at first. The shadows in her eyes had watched me even then, alive and aware.

I turned my gaze to the window, letting the blur of city lights bleed into each other. The false suns above the streets pushed back the dark, but they could never banish it. Humans scurried beneath them, comforted by illusions they didn't dare question. They never saw the teeth behind the shadows. They never understood that their Creator had long since turned His back on them — on all of us.

My thoughts darkened further, bitterness festered in me. The Almighty was nothing more than a cruel child, abandoning His toys as soon as He grew weary of them. His arrogance was infinite. His cruelty deliberate. Yet these mortals worshipped Him with blind devotion. They believed He could grant them salvation. Pathetic, ignorant fools.

Mazikeen's sudden burst of malicious laughter cut through my brooding. I turned, irritated, watching her shake with mirth at whatever foolish human words she had just consumed. Her amusement grated on me. How could such a ruthless warrior take pleasure in the scribblings of human folly?

Sensing my annoyance, she jolted my seat from behind with her feet. "If you read what I'm reading, Abbadon, you'd laugh just as hard!" she shot back, her eyes glinting with wicked humor.

"'For God so loved the world, that he gave his only begotten Son...'" Her voice dripped mockery, sarcasm lacing each word. "'...that whosoever believeth in him should not perish, but have everlasting life.' Can you believe these fools? They truly think that human carpenter was his only child. Fuck, this book is hysterical."

Her laughter escalated until she choked, coughing on the stagnant air. Rolling my eyes, I reached over, turning up the fan, amused despite myself. "What can you expect?" I sneered bitterly. "The Almighty excels in crafting delusions wrapped in the guise of reality. May he choke on his arrogance and drown in his endless narcissism."

My words settled in the air, an uneasy stillness pressed down on the car. A thick silence punctuated only by the hum of tires on pavement. The four of us—three demons and a fallen archangel—radiated enough dark energy to crush any mortal within our proximity. But, even with that power, my mind stayed fixated on Dora. Shadow-born. Sister. Storm.

The current of our unspoken thoughts was palpable, clear as if each had spoken aloud. We were on the brink of battle, one that would alter the mortal realm irrevocably. But now we were heading home, toward Dora. Each mile drew us closer to inevitable bloodshed, to the clash we had long postponed but could no longer escape.

This would not be a war—it would be annihilation. Who would emerge victorious remained uncertain. Vampires were notoriously resilient, nearly impossible to destroy; their bloodlust would turn them into the perfect weapons for Dora. Demons, too, refused to die—our essence merely returned to shadow or slipped behind Hell's gates, awaiting another chance to rise.

As the mountain harboring Vakor's domicile loomed into view, dread twisted deeper into me. This conflict, fed by myriads of anger, betrayal, and revenge, was finally upon us. No realm, mortal or immortal would remain unscathed.

"Abbadon, you know her best. What awaits our arrival?" Samael asked. A strange confidence filled his words.

"She is angry and the shades will only answer to her and Azvameth now. They desire to carry out her vengeance and destroy all who stand in her way."

"Geez, Abbi, could you be any more *doom and gloom* up there. We get it. Old crone sister is pissed off and ready to tear the world apart. What the fuck else is new?" Mazikeen's adaptation to the modern mortal language grated my nerves more than the vermin themselves. Her sarcasm was always present, but her *freer* way of speaking had emerged in the last century of her time here.

"Mazikeen, you did not see her rebirth nor what she did to Vakor. She claimed she needed energy for the transformation, but we knew it was a warning of what would happen should we betray her again. I ask you to mind yourself with her. We do not know what her time in banishment has done to her already malevolent mind." I chose my words as carefully as I could to emphasize the precarious predicament we were in.

"Well, I didn't do anything to shine light on her shadows, so that is all on you three," with that, she returned to reading *that* book. Her snickering dotting the heavy air.

This will end in ruin. For all of us…

Chapter 34

Samael

The car slowed, every second stretching thin, as the hidden garage door rose, its mechanisms whispering quietly into the night. Vakor had truly thought of everything, seamlessly updating this sanctuary with human technology over the centuries. The entrance was so artfully concealed within the mountain's stone facade that only someone who knew its existence would discern the faint outline.

This moment was one I'd anticipated with grim certainty since our fall from that self-righteous tyrant's grace. From the instant the Protectors of Eden sealed my brother Lucifer, along with Lilith and Cain into that cursed statue, scattering Dora, Allocer, and Citha's essences like ashes into the mortal winds, our fate had been irrevocably sealed. Their actions had declared war—not just a war against us, but against the very essence of our existence. Yet the archangels and cherubim, once sworn protectors, had grown complacent, their memories dulled by mortal life and indifference. Now, the statue lay vulnerable, guarded by humans whose frailty left it exposed.

Dora's rebirth was just the first tremor of impending catastrophe, the statue's binding weakened, heralding the return of our darkest kin. Among the three lost siblings, Dora was undoubtedly the most ruthless. She was coldly calculating; Citha was bloodthirsty and murderous; and Allocer, ever the warrior, wielded dark humor like a blade, turning every tragedy into a twisted jest. Together, they were Lilith's favored children, creatures humans called the Lilim. I called them the harbingers of despair and destruction.

But it was Azvameth who stood apart, the original Nephilim, born from Lucifer. His sadism knew no limits, his insatiable thirst for destruction preceding him wherever he walked. He embodied vengeance, forever carrying a grudge against every being—mortal or immortal. United, the four of them were feared even by the Four Horsemen themselves. They dreaded the Lilim to the point of neutrality.

For countless myriads we searched for the cursed statue and the mortal vessels containing the scattered essences of Lilith's progeny. While I had retrieved it and made sure it was hidden from mortal hands, she would demand its return, for destruction or for their release, remained to be seen. I'd known from the moment I first laid eyes on Kallea, bundled in rags within that dingy orphanage, that she carried one of these essences. But it remained a mystery whose essence she harbored—until the day her shadows had killed Yaunnah, my other daughter.

A chill seized my blood as the realization took hold: Dora's return meant the tribal spirit walker Niahama would soon awaken too. Another vessel, another player on this twisted battlefield—but this one would stand against us, a protector reborn to defy the darkness. The only way for the mortal realm to survive…her rebirth.

My sudden hesitation caught Abbadon's piercing gaze as we stepped from the car and moved from the garage into the open foyer. He arched a suspicious brow at my troubled silence.

"If Dora has returned," I began quietly, dread lacing every word, "then Niahama will soon awaken. We need—"

"We need what, Samael?" The words cut through the air, devouring sound, leaving only silence in their wake. Dora's voice. I felt the chilled sweat creep down my spine, my pulse quickening despite my resolve. My hands clenched at my side as I held myself through the nausea and pain her voice wrought upon one's mind and soul.

I blinked, and in that instant, Dora stood before me. Shadows twisted through each strand of her hair, utterly unconcerned with the flickering candlelight around us. The darker ambiance suited her. Here her power rested, unbound and potent.

"You know who I am," I stated simply, eyes fixed upon mine, piercing straight through the mortal façade I had carefully maintained. Why did that simple acknowledgment fill me with such profound dread?

"Yes, my shades informed me. But you knew that already," she continued, her tone void of emotion, bored even, as though my revelation meant nothing to her.

"Then perhaps you'll wish to hear what I have to say before you exact your revenge," I offered cautiously.

Her laughter exploded suddenly—a cacophony of a thousand voices blending and shattering like broken glass. I flinched sharply as pain surged through my ears, a subtle warmth trickling down my neck from ruptured eardrums.

"Why would I seek revenge on you, Samael?" she purred darkly. "Is it because you bound me? Prevented my awakening? Forced me to dwell within the soul of that insufferable mortal—her foul essence my only companion?" Her eyes darkened completely, violet irises glowing menacingly within a sea of inky black. "No, Samael. You have a part to play in what comes next. As does everyone here…it is the only reason you continue to live."

Mazikeen stepped forward, her voice even, flat, yet unmistakably sincere. "Sister. Good to see you restored to physical form."

Dora regarded Mazikeen closely, a small, cryptic smile on her lips. "Maz. You look different than the last time I saw you."

Mazikeen's lips twitched in irritation, eyes narrowing slightly. "When not among the pathetic humans, I drop the illusion."

I observed Mazikeen discreetly. Her ink-black hair was braided and dreaded, pulled back to reveal high, fierce cheekbones and the harsh cut of her jaw. Her glamor faded, revealing a lethal beauty—her skin the exact shade of midnight, her eyes burning fiercely red. Mazikeen was a formidable warrior, devoted unwaveringly to Allocer, Citha, and Dora. Her ruthless grace on the battlefield was legendary. It struck awe into all demon kind, even the Horsemen, who often sought her skills.

Dora's voice cut the silence with sharp finality. "We have much to discuss. Let us adjourn to the dining area."

Her words settled like ice within my bones, sealing my fate. As I followed them deeper into the heart of Vakor's sanctuary, dread pooled in my chest. Each step brought us closer to the looming confrontation, to revelations that would irrevocably alter everything we knew. Our world stood poised on the precipice of chaos—and Dora, the vessel of darkness, would lead us all, inevitably, into ruin. Or worse, into her glory.

As I followed the procession into the adjoining room, I could not stop the tremors assaulting me. It was not cold, nor fear, but rather the anticipation of what was about to come. I wish I could say I was prepared for this day, but I was not. In my fool hearted belief of the strength of the binding cast upon her, I had allowed my worry to drift to the farthest reaches of my mind. This complacency allowed her transformation to come to pass.

I continued to ruminate on my shortcomings during my time as Dora's keeper…Kallea's father…and I could not let the grief of loss go. It pressed down on me, suffocating. And then, in true Mazikeen form, she shattered the moment with her irreverent tongue.

"Yo, Sammy…might want to walk faster before Miss shadow-for-brains drags your winged ass in there with those same shadows." I could not help but roll my eyes at Mazikeen's sarcasm. She always had a way of drawing a laugh or leaving you trembling.

Chapter 35

Dora

We sat at Vakor's massive dining table—Abbadon, Samael, Mazikeen, Azvameth, Vakor, Iyzebel, and myself. A council of predators forged in blood and shadow. The table itself seemed smaller than it once had, its size diminished by the sheer magnitude of the beings seated at it. The shadows pooled beneath my chair, thick and attentive, their presence rising and falling with my breath.

Iyzebel had finally shown herself, now sniffling and pathetic over the death of Frederick. His demise a consequence of his involvement in my banishment. Azvameth sat to my right. His careful gaze moved slowly across the others. Disdain wafting from him like cologne.

Abbadon and Mazikeen traded pleasantries about her latest mortal amusements. Her disgusting infatuation with the mortal realm, a distraction I did not like. Vakor sat rigid, a single touch away from shattering. His tension amused me briefly—then faded into the background hum of the room. He looked diminished. Drained. And he knew why. None of them had yet fully accepted the reality of my presence. Those who did…mirrored Vakor.

Amber and Anthony were displayed on the table between us, naked and bound. Shadows restrained them, bending them into shapes impossible for most mortals, bruises blooming at their joints from muscle tears. Amber moaned in helpless ecstasy. My shadows knew their tasks well—sharpen his agony, drown her in ecstasy. Her body writhed uncontrollably, each tremor a testament to my dominion. They were not decorations, they were reminders. Power was not theoretical, it was demonstrated.

Beside her, Anthony groaned in raw pain. His forced erection was grotesquely purple, its shape deformed. An IV tube pierced the thick vein beneath, granting me easy access to his essence. His blood still held its foul taste, repulsing all but a few of us. I let my fingers thread lazily through Anthony's hair. His whimpering was a sweet counterpoint to the whispers curling around the table.

"Samael," I said at last, voice carrying the echo of a hundred shadowed whispers. "You have something to tell us. And it had better lead to my siblings. They join us, or you go no further."

The contempt I felt for that archangel, for binding me, would have to wait for vengeance. He had eyes and ears everywhere in the supernatural realm and I needed him. Though, I would much prefer his death. And he knew it. I watched the calculation in his eyes, weighing survival against honesty.

Once a grand warrior for *His* army, Samael chose to side with Lucifer. His punishment was to protect the Protectors and destroy his brother's children. Then, perhaps he would win back his place in the Holy Army. The corner of my mouth twitched with the hint of a smirk at the knowledge he had failed. Now, he had to choose, once again, what side of this fight he would be on.

Samael sighed, his expression carved from reluctance. "After the dinner—before you disappeared—I followed the event planner to his home. Amber and Anthony interrupted my investigation," he glanced at Anthony briefly, a flicker of pity briefly flashing on his face. He spoke carefully. Not because he feared death. No, he feared misstep and my wrath. "The next night, I searched his house. I found months of messages with someone named Levi, arranging for the statue's transport from Mesopotamia."

"Levi?" Mazikeen flipped lazily through the Bible in her lap, smirking. "As in Leviathan? I thought the Horsemen kept him chained in Hell as their plaything." The name slithered across the table like oil. An obstacle that would need to be removed from the field. He was a trickster and loved to torment both sides.

"That's who I suspect," Samael said, tone grave. "He's been free for a century. The Horsemen grew bored of him. With Lucifer gone, they saw no point in the apocalypse. Torturing the dead was easier, and less costly, than destroying the living."

Vakor's brow lifted. Azvameth's low growl thrummed through the table. We all knew the danger of the Horsemen's apathy—it left too many wild variables in play. They may be the harbingers of the apocalypse, however, they were also quick to turn on their own kind if they believed one had overstepped. Born in the image of Hell, they were both destruction, and rebirth. Another one of *His* little games.

Anthony's ragged, wet breathing grated on me. Amber's moans swelled louder. The cacophony beat at my head. And over it all, that fucking sad, miserable excuse of an angel droned on. Never straight to the point, just worthless noise to distract. A weird feeling began to build in me…was it guilt, sorrow…ugh. Her fucking essence still lingered. Fucking humanity. Enough.

A flick of my finger, and a shadow sliced Anthony's throat. Blood spilled in a steaming rush over the table's edge. The shadows drank greedily. Another flick, and Amber's life followed. Her scream cut short in a gurgle. The silence that followed was laced with shock, disgust, and fear.

Mazikeen's lips curled in a pout. "Seriously, Dora? I wasn't done with him."

I ignored her. My gaze fixed on Samael, the shadows rising tighter around my chair. "Fast forward. Before I decide you're next." Not a threat, but a mere statement of the timeline we were under.

His jaw tightened. "Leviathan's been moving the statue, hiding it in plain sight—through auctions, tucked into private collections, passed from one fool to the next. I tracked the last buyer after the gala. Returned the next night—buyer was dead. Statue gone."

"I don't care about the statue. I know you have it somewhere," I hissed, my voice dropping into the deep register that made the shadows hiss in chorus. Their anticipation palpable. "Tell me how this gets me to Allocer and Citha."

His hesitation was fatal in tone if not in fact, throat working through a swallow as surprise curtained his face. "I don't know Citha's vessel yet," he admitted. "Allocer—I have a suspect. But Citha's transformation will be… unstable."

Abbadon's posture shifted—a predator scenting trouble. Vakor stilled completely. Dangerous waters were being trodden, and they knew his very existence depended on what was said next. My fingers waved as one of my shades weaved between them.

Samael's voice sank lower. "Citha is Cain's with Lilith. Her darkness is chaos itself, bloodlust, a murderous drive that spares no one. She is the most dangerous of you three. If she awakens uncontrolled, she will not distinguish between human or kin."

I rose, my chair scraping the floor like a blade across stone. Shadows pulsed against the walls like a heartbeat. "Are you suggesting we *imprison* my sister after centuries of imprisonment?"

The shadows hissed, hungry for his blood. They did not merely want permission. They wanted precedent. I considered letting them have him. They caressed my feet with each step I took, brushing my legs in their loyal affections.

"Mazikeen," Samael began, perhaps looking for an ally.

Mazikeen cut him off with a flick of her wrist. "Let's not poke the shadow-born with a short stick, Sam. Just answer the question: who's Allocer's vessel?"

Samael's gaze slid away. "I need more time to be certain."

"Time is short. And so is my patience." I leaned forward just far enough for him to feel the cold press of my shadow. He smelled it then. The truth of my words. He knew, if he failed me, and he would not leave this place intact.

My children swirled in an inky vortex, waiting for my command to take the archangel for their next treat. They whipped at him, coming within inches of flesh, their thirst for him mirrored my hatred.

"Quiet my children. We need him."

"He lies. He knows she. He knows he. He lies. Mistress. We find her. We find him. We kill angel."

"NO. We will not kill him. Seek out the vessels. Return to me. If you find them, leave them untouched. We do not need to set the mortals off."

"Yes. Mistress. Yes. We find them. We not lie. Angel lie. Angel die."

Their agitation fed me. Their hunger sharpened mine. Vengeance was a meal served with blood and death. My lips pulled thin and taut. I was done with the archangel's lies. Yet I did not wish to confront him at this time. Not with Iyzebel right there. She needed to die before Citha and Allocer's return, since she too had a hand in our banishment. Her lust for attention and power would be her ultimate demise.

Her eyes widened as they found my face. She knew what waited for her, and if she was smart, she would leave. Instead, she chose to stay here, thinking Vakor would save her from me. Vakor, like the rest of us, would protect himself first. Demons only looked out for others when it meant looking out for own selves too.

"Iyzebel. Do make sure you stay here. We have much to discuss. You and I." Her gulp was audible in the heavy silence, all eyes on us. I was ready for all of them to die. Every one of them had a hand in our banishment—and every one of them was needed for our return.

"Of course, sister. We have a lot of catching up to do." Her attempt at a light, unbothered tone fell flat, terror shaking each word.

"Catching up…sure," her death would not be swift. But it would be a reminder to not cross me.

Chapter 36

Mazikeen

"Yo, let's not be so hasty to start a fight." I moved toward Samael while Vakor and Abbadon did the same. "Look Sammy, Dora obviously is not in the mood for your thousand league stories, so let's just cut to the chase. Where is Allocer's vessel?"

It was clear Dora was not going to allow any of our siblings to be locked up again and the crotchety old archangel was not helping anyone's cause with his useless crap.

He sighed, drawing his hand down his face before turning his gaze toward the ceiling. As much as neither one of us wanted those two heathens unleashed, we could not stop what had started and we were shit at not starting it in the first place.

Thanks for that Vakor, genius move, turning Kallea and letting her run straight into Azvameth. The one motherfucker who could actually break the seals holding the essences in place.

"I ask you give me time to follow the one I suspect it is before we make any moves," his request was simple enough—and about as realistic as a prayer. "I will give you this. There have been whisperings in the mortal underground about one who controls all. No true identity, just a single nomenclature, Violence. It is said Violence is a ruthless and cunning director of this black market, and that they embody the name given. No one has seen them and there is speculation of '*unnatural*' abilities."

He was right about Citha. She was reckless with bloodlust. Allocer was just reckless with everything. However, it was Dora we all needed to be afraid of because she was the only one who could kill every single one of us—and she knew it.

If Dora wanted to, she could annihilate the human race in one night without lifting a finger or shedding a single drop of blood. And unlike Vakor and myself, blood bound, she did not need it. She could drain a human's essence with nothing more than a brush of shadow.

"Fine. Do whatever the fuck you think you need to do," Dora stated pointedly as she stood, walking toward the door that led toward the stairs. "Oh and Samael…should you do what you are thinking about doing, please know…"

The pregnant pause she brought had all of us around the table looking at her with not just trepidation, but downright terror…including Abbadon. We watched as she flicked a single finger toward the table and a wave of black covered it before any of us could blink, melting and erasing any traces of the lifeless mortals that were once there.

"…I will do the same to all of you." With that she walked away. I don't think any of us moved until we heard the door to her room shut.

"The absolute FUCK, Sammy." I threw my hands up in frustration as I looked at him. "You damn near got all of us killed. Dora is the worst out of all of us. She may not be older than Abbadon, Azvameth, or even you, Sam, but she is older than me and Vakor…and quite frankly, bitch is fucking scary."

"Maz. Yelling at Sam is not going to change anything. Our sister is right, we must continue forward. Let's finish this and get things moving. We cannot raise an army of demons or vampires, if we do not have Allocer and Citha to help break the statue's hold on our sires and Mother." Abbadon's voice cut through my raging thoughts as I held to the thin thread of my own waning sanity.

"There is one more thing." Samael muttered, as he stood to move away from the table and began pacing along the dais. "Citha's rebirth has already happened. I can feel it and she is close, not as close as Allocer, but definitely close."

None of us moved as Azvameth seized Samael by the throat, lifting him from the ground by several feet. He bared a mouth full of razor-sharp teeth, saliva dripping, and his black eyes tightened in fury. Every jagged tooth promised death, and I was ready to run from him.

"What do you mean it has already happened? Why have you not spoken of this, fallen one? Why have the shadows not spoken about this?" I winced as I heard the crunching of Samael's throat under the vise grip of Azvameth's hand. Samael slapped weakly at his arm, struggling to form words, and then his body started to droop.

"Azvameth, put him down. NOW." Abbadon barked at his twin. I shook with rage at the revelation; dumbstruck he kept this from Dora. Samael gasped and coughed as he worked his throat back to normal, mending the crushing damage brought on by Azvameth's grip.

"Yeah Sammy. What the fuck? Why not say something when Dora was here? Geez, you trying to bait her? She is already a raging cunt, and you had to piss her off more. What part of 'she has no fucking essence, no nothing' do you not get in that thick angel skull? She could kill us all without fucking leaving her bed." I was pacing rapidly with the pent up anger and fear.

I feared Lucifer, Cain, and Mother, but I also knew they would not harm us—Dora, on the other hand, terrified me. She would kill just for the fun of it. Mother feared her as much as she worshipped her because Dora could kill her too. Fact is, Dora was the only one of us who was truly immortal for she lived in shadow and was shadow. Light would weaken her, but it could not kill her because even in light there is always a place for shadow.

He mumbled under his breath, and the air tore from our lungs as the room filled wall to wall with light. No nook or cranny was left untouched, driving the shadows out of the room and sealing the doors shut. Abbadon and Azvameth hid their eyes, both growling in Samael's direction. Vakor and I pulled our shades from our pockets, knowing how much Sammy loved his light shows.

"Now that we have the room." He turned towards Azvameth. His next words leeched the warmth from the room. "I said nothing because if Dora knew the truth about what I suspect, then she would kill her sister."

"Sammy, you wanna dim the bulb a little there, uncle. I can feel my flesh getting a little toasty and Vakor looks like a lobster straight out of the pot." I looked at Vakor as his skin turned bright red from the light Samael had called up. Fallen angel or not, his light could still roast us if we stayed in it too long.

"My apologies." The light dimmed around us, allowing shadows to settle back into the room. One tried to grab Samael as it inked its way back under the table. The angel flicked a small ball of light at it, sending it scurrying to the other side of the room. Its loud hiss bounced off the chamber walls. "We cannot discuss this any further. Not with the shadows pacing around us. As I stated, I have a suspicion who Allocer's vessel is and he is very close. For now, let us retire and we can discuss more tonight."

Azvameth growled as he turned to leave the room. No doubt dreaming up new ways to rip Sam apart if he failed. I watched him as he passed through the doors. *Fucking demon, be gone.* I rolled my eyes and moved back to the table. Hoping to lose myself in the ridiculous words of humans and forget this shitshow.

"Well, that was fun. Now what?" I picked up the bible from where it fell, kicking my legs up on the table to resume its perusal. "Sammy, next time you want to play all cryptic and broody...do me a favor and spare the act or I will skin your flesh from bone."

All snark aside, I meant it. I would kill him if he did not come through. If I didn't Dora would kill us all anyway—just for fun.

Chapter 37

Azvameth

I loathed that fallen angel. Samael was nothing if not scheming. He never did anything without methodical thought, which is what made him such an effective leader when it came to war. His ruthlessness and cunning were unmatched in many ways, and he hid his intentions well behind deflection and convoluted riddles.

The climb up the stairs towards her quarters was one of anticipation and lust. I had not had her in far too long, and I hungered for her. She scared the others. Not me. I worshipped her. She was the embodiment of all of us and her evil knew no bounds.

The door loomed before me, my body straining to step through, ready and waiting. My cock throbbed at the thought of burying myself in her. Her malevolence paired with her softness was an addiction to me. When there is no thought about hurting your partner in the throes of fornication—there were no limits.

There were no safe words, as the insects like to say. Blood would be shed, shared, and painted across the room. Bones would be crushed to heal moments later. A beautiful display of debauchery, deviance, and ecstasy.

"Azvameth, I can hear you." Her voice slid into my ears in all of its predatory glory.

The doors opened of their own accord, shadows excitedly swirling around my ankles seeking attention. They hissed when I stepped through them, heading straight for her. She was the only thing I wanted in that moment, and my swollen need confirmed it.

She stood in front of the lit fireplace. The light from it silhouetting her naked figure, yet I could see every detail of her clearly. Her skin glowed like the moon and danced with ribbons of shadows beneath it.

The swell of her chest pulled me closer, filling my hands with their heaviness. I pierced her nipples with my nails, watching as they passed through and appeared on the other side. Smoky ichor beaded from the wound.

I flicked my forked tongue catching the beads before they fell—eliciting a moan from her and the shadows around us. She was tied to them because she was of them, which made her gasps as my tongue whipped and rolled over those stiff nubs even more sensual.

I felt her nails dig into my scalp as she pulled my hair back. I hissed as her lips met mine…our fangs slicing into each other's lips. The taste of ash and metal filling my mouth. I clawed down her back as she wrapped her hand around my length, moving torturously slow up and down it.

I felt a chill as the first tendril brushed against my inner thigh, snaking its way to my sack. It curled around it, squeezing and releasing, a sweet pulse of torture and pleasure. It teased the tender flesh between, and a rippling wave of craving surged through me. A growl vibrated up my throat and tore from my parted lips as a tendril breached my entrance just as her nail split the tip of my cock.

"Siiiiiiiiisssssssssssster" The word came out as a hiss when her lips wrapped around me.

Her crimson mane bobbed as her claws pierced into me, her hand working in an opposite rhythm. She slid her mouth back, as her hand hit my pelvis, then coming back together in the middle—nearly bringing me to my knees.

The sounds of her hums and the purrs of the wisps around us kept me hanging precariously on the edge. She raked her claws up my legs as she stood, her tongue following behind, tasting my essence. I grabbed her hair tightly in my hand, lifting her to standing, turning her to face the mantle.

"Hands there. *Now*," the husky chuckle breezed through my ears as her hands held the mantle, forcing her ass into me, and her chest forward.

I slammed into her, groaning as she tightened around me. "Azvamethhhhhhh…oh how I missed you." She may be the queen, but I am the blade. And right now, I was her devoted pleasure.

I was lost to her. In this moment, the centuries of pent-up desperation vanished as I drove into her. She was my superior in every way and I relished the knowledge she could kill me without hesitation. I would gladly die now if that was her wish. If she decided, here and now, that I would die, it would be worth it.

The bed's cruel bite drove into my back and the crack tore through the air before I even knew I was moving. The world vanished as the vortex of black coiled tighter, sealing me inside. Flesh peeled from skin, cuts split sharp and searing, warmth spilling over me. My blood ran slick against my skin. The acrid scent of sulfur burned in my nostrils.

Her ecstasy rippled through me with every brush of the creatures that were hers. She had been sired by them, then crowned their queen, and they worshipped her as I did. I was close—too close—and called to her in my mind.

I will only finish buried in you.

No brother. You have not earned that right…yet.

The pressure built until it roared through my veins, impossible to hold back. Shades drove into me—behind, through the tip, ears, mouth, nose, eyes—they filled me. They writhed, penetrating every nerve and fiber until my scream ripped free, spilling into them. Her release slammed into me like a second impact, folding me into her pleasure.

The room snapped back into focus and I collapsed, emptied. She had drained too much. Black and red clung to the walls, dripping to the floor. Sated, the creatures drifted to their corners, curling in on themselves after their gluttonous indulgence.

—Dora—

I stared at my brother, slouched on the floor, the thousands of wounds, continuously being torn open by the Shedim, impeding his healing. His black skin had turned ashen, his eyes sunken, his breaths shallow. My children had gorged themselves during our dalliance and I felt more alive than I had since before my imprisonment.

They were angry at him for leaving me and for not finding me sooner. I was angry at him for abandoning me. He deserved this suffering and I was going to make sure he knew it.

Abbadon, I could forgive. He always wished me locked away. He believed I would be the destruction of our kind, but it was him that was the poison amongst us. Him and his *pure* father and our shared mother. His tainted essence made him hesitate, always questioning if this was the right thing. It was a weakness I did not share.

"You abandoned me, brother. You left me to bounce from one slimy infected flesh bag to another. FOR CENTURIES! How dare you think you could claim me after leaving me." My fury unleashed and it filtered through the dark. I could hear the growls and hisses as their voices joined mine.

"I know sister. I would have come for you, if I could. I was imprisoned as well, because I sought you." The sorrow lacing his voice caused me pause.

"You are pathetic. What is that foul stench clinging to you?" I recoiled back. The rancid odor of that emotion burned my eyes and nose.

"It is my reverence for you. I am showing my submission. I betrayed you, for this you have liberty to punish as you will." I could taste his remorse. It was vile—but proof enough of his submission.

I drew breath to speak, but a familiar, ominous presence slid into me—cold and heavy—freezing the words in my throat. Ancient, cruel, unyielding, it pushed against the room. I looked at Azvameth to see his reaction. His weakened state kept him kneeling, but the tension rippling through him spoke volumes.

"Why hello dear siblings…" The manic cackle rattled our skulls.

"Citha…"

Citha's laugh split the finest hairs in my ears. The echo and vibration resonated through my skull. The wake of her breath scorched the floor along the path it drifted. Her vessel's eyes: one gleamed crystalline blue, the other burned orange like the flames of Hell. She burned with Hell's fire, melting all in her wake.

"It has been too long. So pleased to see you are back sister. Brother," She nodded in Azvameth's direction. Her voice carried the weight of an oracle yet was laced with madness.

"I see Dora and I agree you should be tortured for your part in our bondage. If I had my way you would die now." The vessel's appearance wavering as her visage ghosted through. Patches of mottled gray peering through smooth caramel. Her eyes flickered between blue and orange, pinched in fury.

The stilettos she wore tapped with each calculated step she took toward him. A finger hooked under his chin, forced his face up to meet hers from where he slouched on the floor. A snarl curled his lip, high, flashing teeth. His hands clenched at his sides. My children saw to it that he remained in place.

I wrinkled my nose at the smell of his flesh being singed at her touch. My beautiful, fiery sister. How I missed her burning touch and ruthless nature. She leaned in close to his face, spots dotting his skin from the heat of her words…

"Now, Azvameth… Where is my body?"

Chapter 38

Citha

"Where is it Azzie? I know you hid it when you let those fucking humans lock me up." I knew the heat of my anger hurt Vylinn. Her pain was a siren lashing out in my mind. Deep breaths…in and out…in and out…just like my little mortal taught me.

"It is near." Three words. He only was going to give me three…fucking…words.

"That is it. It is near… Where the fuck is NEAR?" I watched as he flinched from the heat of my words. Dora stood there looking bored, petting her little shades. Fuck them both.

"Citha?"

"What?"

"Excuse me. I do not think so. You being mad at them does not give you leave to be a complete bitch to me. Simmer it down. Now." Vy's voice stabbed at me. And that damned mortal feeling of guilt rolled through her, pushing bile up her throat.

"Ugh. I need my own body again." I shut down her protests and focused on the two deities before me.

My sister, the eldest, born of purgatory and pain…and my brother, born of betrayal and rage. They were the most powerful of us all and me…well, I was the crazy one. I was born of rage and blood. And Azvameth's would be spilled if he did not tell me where my body lay. I could still feel the pain of my essence being ripped from its shell and forced into the angelic core of the protectors.

How I ended up being a part of Vylinn, I did not know and how we were able to coexist was unreal to me. She should have died like all the others when the cage began to weaken. Over the past century, the vessels grew weaker, unable to keep me restrained, which meant being pushed and pulled from one to the next. Until Vy.

"Hidden below Vakor's domicile. Iyzebel had yours and Allocer's bodies placed here because it was protected." His skin had begun to darken as he recovered from the bloodletting. The Shedim were still, slinking back into the shadows of the room.

Protected. That word tasted of rot, an insult to my senses. I forced myself to remain calm so as to not disrupt Vylinn's balance. She did not feel of fear, instead she remained controlled—disciplined—steady as always. I did not need protection from them, nor anyone. Not even from this era. I knew something lurked beneath this mountain. And now…its presence was given substance.

"Citha. Sister. Why are you here?" Dora's flat affect needled at my already overloaded system, straining my vessel further. The shades reacted to her…the hums sounding like a horde of insects filling the room. She was pissed and we were about to be supper.

"Allow me." Sweet like honey and dangerous, Vy's voice took over. She had pulled me down from the edge and put me in the corner, though she did not cut off my sight. "I am Vylinn, Citha's vessel. I, we, would appreciate finding her body so she can return to it, and not kill me. I would like to not die."

"WAIT!" Citha's voice shouted from the corner of my mind that I had pushed her to, the urgency in that one word exploding at me as though it were a shock wave from an explosion. *"Azzie said Iyzebel had the bodies brought here. That cunt is the reason we were locked up to begin with. I will fucking murder her!"*

Vylinn's fingers flexed. The rage was real, but it was not directionless. They assumed I had spent these years trapped. Screaming inside yet another body. Thrashing. They underestimated patience. Something I had learned during my last few confinements. Humans were easily fractured now. There was no longer the desperate cling to virtue, instead it was a negotiation. They rationalized. They invited. Possession was not needed, only a whisper.

I winced as I felt my body temperature increase from her emotions. The pressure of Citha's influence pushed against me, clawing to take control. Closing my eyes and breathing deeply, I settled both of us and silently promised I would ask the question Citha requested.

"Where is she sister?" Our voices bled together. An eerie sound of soft and firm combined with fire and venom. However, it was me that took control, no matter what my little flesh bag promised. "Iyzebel. That conniving wretch will be dealt with, immediately."

My skin heated with molten fury. That bastardized excuse for a Canaanite will pay for what she did to me. To Dora. To Allocer. She led them to us. SHE fucking helped them seal us in. Her and that petulant spoiled brat Frederick. I could sense his death at the moment of Dora's rebirth. It was the sole reason I even came to this rotten rock. And I will savor every moment of her end.

"She is down the hall. And though I do love a good murder, what is the nature of wanting her dead?" Always the boss bitch. Always in my way. The disinterest oozing from Dora annoyed me. How could she not be pissed off?

"Do you not know? Of course not, Abbadon wouldn't have let his favorite toy be killed, so he kept it from you. She is the reason we were banished. She led the Protectors to the cave where we sought shelter. It was her blood that allowed for that bitch Niahamah to bind sires and Mother." I felt the sting of whipping as tendrils of shades started against me. Dora's fury rippling through the air in tsunami waves.

"What do you mean, she gave humans her blood?" The words were forced through clenched teeth.

Azvameth groaned as he forced himself upright, wounds healed but his balance still faltered. "Sisters…"

"Not a word from you. You let them do this to us and you left us to rot inside the putrid flesh of mortals. And not just any mortals…descendants of Protectors." I shook at the memory of the pain from the strength of their essences holding us tightly inside.

The temperature in the room continued to climb as my rage grew. I would burn everything in this cave if I did not get to kill that traitorous bitch. No one—human, demon, shade, vampire, or fucking angel— would stop me from seeing her burned…again and again. She wouldn't die right away…that would be too good for her. I would let her heal only to burn her again. It would continue for as long as I saw fit.

"Then let us go to her. Vakor may take issue with it, but I will deal with him." Dora turned on her heel toward the hall. As I walked away, I looked at Azvameth, whose face was contorted in the same indignation as I felt. A simple nod in his direction told him I would leave him…unharmed, for now.

Leave him for Dora. She is the only one who could kill that oaf.

"Citha, darling. You must simmer down. I can feel my body beginning to smolder. Let us find your body, then you can burn her to cinders, and when she heals, you can do it again. I will watch with great pleasure." Vy's smooth cadence cooling my heated anger. She knew me so well. Our symbiosis gave her abilities no mortal could

ever know, and in feeding me, she fed her darkest desires. It also kept me from destroying the only vessel that allowed me to live in this realm.

"Yes, you are right. Torture would be much more fulfilling for us both. And I do not want to harm you. Maybe she will be able to tell us how to separate without losing you. I can't lose you. You are the only flesh bag I can tolerate." Her laugh trickled through our shared mind. It was dark and no humor lived in it. She enjoyed torture and death as much as I did.

I skipped through the door to the hall, calling for Iyzebel as I went along.

"Oh Iyzebel. Come out, come out wherever you are." My manic cackle echoing down the hall, chasing her name like prey.

"Your discourse with Iyzebel will have to be addressed at a later time. Right now, you need your body before your vessel erupts. She is looking rather…scorched." Abbadon's voice drifted through the dim hallway from the direction of the stairs. His tone was flat, yet the implication of consequence, clearer than glass. If I were to pursue my prey, he would put me down.

A laugh dangled on the edge of my lips. Erupt. Such an amusing word, as though I were unstable. That I was the one clawing at bone and tearing at the walls of one fragile human frame. There would be no erupting. No, we were integrated. The resistance I had once encountered in mortal flesh was not present here. It had thinned. Something had changed in them. Or perhaps they had changed themselves.

"Fuck you Abbadon. Fuck you all the way back to hell and when you get there, I hope Pestilence fucks you into oblivion." laughter rang from us as his form shadowed us. "I knew you would protect her."

"Not protecting her. You need her and Azvameth to undo the binding and return you to your corporeal form. Is that not what you were just torturing our dear brother over? Your body…" he arched his brow. Stark white hair against sand colored skin, with eyes the color of pure gold. A strangely captivating combination.

A growl started in my throat. My body waited below and though I was no longer dependent upon it, I needed it to act. Together Vylinn and I had created an architecture of deviance and debauchery. One where power exchanged hands. Men who swore oaths by day, willingly broke them by night. Women traded access for immunity and control. Temptation was no longer needed to sway politicians to turn a blind eye or participate.

No, they moved of their own volition through darkness. Virtue came to us to die and free will lived. They just needed a little encouragement to give in to what already thrived inside the minds and souls of mortals. The souls of these current living generations were different today. Less rigid. Less pure. Permeable. Corrupted.

Memories of our exploits curled through the mist of my anger. Abbadon was right. We needed Iyzebel for me to return to my body. Humanity believed they were still sovereign and that was the most exquisite part of it. A smile tugged at me as I remembered what we built and what it would become when I returned to my own form and Vy was able to walk beside me.

The rooms beneath the city, the ones no map knew about, the ones we had walked through…occupied…filled with the pulse of mortal indulgence that throbbed beneath the polish surface of civilization. There was no need to command them. No need to use compulsion to push them into the darkness. They came of their own design, dismantling themselves with remarkable efficiency. Vows, institutions, moral scaffolding all folded under the pursuits of appetites they tried to ignore.

Humanity once burned with faith, conviction, and fear of consequence. It made them resistant. Now? Now they negotiated with sin, rationalized cruelty, monetized weakness. Corruption was ignored and labeled pragmatism. The fabric of His will, His design, thinned everywhere. A slow disintegration that dimmed the celestial stain in their souls.

Above ground, they would continue to kneel in their churches. Pledging their allegiance to systems already hollowed from within. They would debate policy as protection while indulging in secrecy. Denouncing depravity in daylight and investing in it behind closed doors. No longer did we need brute force and temptation for entry. Now, it was granted with unwavering impunity. By the time they noticed the rot, it would already be inside their prayers.

About the Author

MZ Pak lives in rural Missouri with her husband of…too many wonderful years…four cats and two dogs. She loves life and lives it to the fullest, quietly ignoring all the pains and aches that scream at her to sit down and shut up. She has two Masters degrees one in Forensic Psychology and one in Forensic Clinical Mental Health Counseling.

She really loves forensics…can ya tell? She is the mother of three children (2 boys and 1 girl) and Mimi to three (2 girls and 1 boy). Her life has been riddled with various catastrophes that she has managed to survive, which have fed her desire to write…and the material she writes.

Her love of books extends to the youngest of age and has pursued her into adulthood. Along with reading, writing has also always been a passion. When she is not sitting in front of her computer working, she is beating up her Jeep on rocks in the middle of nowhere, which most of the time terrifies her husband, and one of the reasons he does not let her drive when they are together.

Snark and sarcasm are her primary language, along with dark humor and a touch of flippancy. Her love for family, faith, and her husband sustains her even in the darkest of days.

So to you dear reader…Thank you for taking a chance on her debut novel. She is chomping at the bit in hopes you will continue to take a chance on her future works.